CONSIDERING WOMAN I & II

ALSO BY VELMA POLLARD

Poetry
Crown Point
Shame Trees Don't Grow Here
The Best Philosophers I Know Can't Read or Write
Leaving Traces

Fiction
Karl and Other Stories
Homestretch
Considering Woman

Non-fiction
Dread Talk: The Language of Rastafari
From Creole to Standard

ACKNOWLEDGMENTS

Parables (I, II, III) appeared in *Caribbean Quarterly*; Cages in *Bim*; "My Mother" and "Gran" in *Jamaica Journal*; "The Sisters" in *Arts Review*. "My Mother" also appeared in *Over Our Way* (D'Costa and Pollard, editors, Longman 1980) and a translation of "Gran" appeared in *De moedervleksuite* (Ineke Phaf, editor, Het Wereldvenster, 1987); "Ruthless at Noon" appeared as "Nicely" in *Bearing Witness 3, Jamaica Observer*, edited by Wayne Brown; "Smile (God Loves You)" appeared in *Blue Latitudes*, Seal Press edited by Elizabeth Nunez and Jennifer Sparrow; "Glean(h)er" appeared in *MaComère* Volume 3; "Grannany" appeared in *Gulf Coast,* Vol. 18, No. 2; "On my way to somewhere of course" appeared in *New Mango Season* Vol. 2 No. 1.

VELMA POLLARD

CONSIDERING WOMAN I & II

PEEPAL TREE

First published in Great Britain in 2010
Peepal Tree Press Ltd
17 King's Avenue
Leeds LS6 1QS
England

Considering Woman (I) was first published
by The Women's Press in 1989

ISBN13: 9781845231699

Supported by
ARTS COUNCIL
ENGLAND

CONSIDERING WOMAN I

Bitter Tales

On the Way to Somewhere of Course

Better Tales

CONSIDERING WOMAN I

For my granddaughter Stephanie Andrienne and in
memory of my mother Lucy Arabella

WOMEN POETS (WITH YOUR PERMISSION)

the little man
too early home today
surprised me scribbling
while the washer turned
ahaa… I see you
take your little write
well let me see your book…
mhmm… mhmm… not bad not bad
a little comma here
a period there
that sentence can make sense…
almost

your friend there scribbling too
and Genie down the road
well well how nice
how triply nice
not mad not mad…

December 1979

VERSION

and behold Adam he came home early
for in the river where he went to fish
there were no fish
and in the caves where he did go to hunt
there were no bison there
and he called "Eev"

but Eve she couldn't answer
for Eve she didn't hear
so poor old Adam leaned
his bow and arrow on a tree
and with a little search
found Eve
cross legged
dipping sticks
yes slender sticks
in gobie bowls
of purple jamoon blood
and scratching
scratching furiously
the underside
of ekru almond leaves

hey Eve
what's that you doing there
but poor old Eve she clutched the leaf
and hid it underneath her fig
no Adam nothing, nothing Man…
but Adam saw and Adam curious
would see more…
and so she gave the satchel up

lines lines milady
what is this
turned poet… woman… well
amen so let it be

O Adam
make me poet please
and not no wo-man poet
let me be free
and gender-
less dear Ad…

At this point I stopped Eaves-dropping

December 1979

PARABLES

My grandmother had a log in her yard. Not any little kemps of wood you know; a big, long log in her backyard. And from I know myself she always rest her wash-pan on it to wash clothes.

One Monday, just after the school bell ring in the distance and you know that children get recess-time, I stay in the house where I was sewing and hear my grandmother give out one scream; one bad scream like she see duppy. I fly outside and see the old lady with her two hands on her cotta and her eyes pulp out like she dead; and when I follow her eyes I see that the wash-pan pitch over and all the clothes on the ground and the scrubbing-board fling to one side and the big, long, old log as old as my time easing itself in a snake walk along an invisible line through the dry ackee leaves and the leaves making a shrr shrr as the slow movement touch them.

One end of the log was little higher than the rest and curved ever so slightly. How come we never noticed that curve all the time? How come we never notice it was a snake before? I could only clap my hand over my mouth and I know for sure my eyes pulp out too. Then I ran outside and called everybody out the road.

What kind of bad-minded snake that, that could sit down for all these years, fool people that it is log; make us wash on it, talk round it, invite we friends to sit down on it, take it make prekkeh in every kind of way, then after all this time, decide to make a move? Mind you, is true the snake didn't threaten anybody; is true nobody even try to find out if is a poison snake; and it didn't run, it only moved, v-e-r-y slowly.

Somebody had the presence of mind in all the general confusion, to run to the police station and phone the zoo and after a while the zoo people came with their kind of ambulance. You should see the crowd by the time they come! Next thing I know the snake was in a coil shape like an oversized rope and I couldn't see over the tall men's head how they get the poor unresisting thing into their vehicle.

The snake had moved, and everybody vex. Long after the ambulance gone, people telling the story with vexation to anybody who didn't pass at the first scream or two. Such a commotion and for so long the poor ackee tree must be wonder what happen; must wonder if they upside-down the world…

A man was seen walking down the street with the head of his wife dripping blood on his khaki pants. The head was tucked firmly under his arm. Huge tears rolled from the creased-up corners of his eyes and he wailed loud and deep all the time looking with reproach at the hapless head:

"Look what you mek me do! Look what you mek me do."

My miserable Auntie, the one who always look like she dreaming, used to walk with her right hand cup halfway as if she constantly holding something; and since we always say, "Cho, she mad," I never ask her what she was carrying till the day after she come back from two months with Aunt B and I notice her hand keeping straight straight at her side like everybody else.

"Aunt May, what happen to you hand?" I ask her.

"How you mean, what happen to mi han?"

"You hand look straight. Not that same right hand you used to cup all the time since we small?"

She said, "Shhh. Listen, but don't laugh." And she look round to see if anybody hearing. Then she start talk to me softly and say:

"You see, is a little child I was carrying right in my hand middle; small you know. One little beeny pickny; like one of dem jumping frogs; only plenty smaller; and every now and then if a take me eye off it, when I look again it shrink; and if I walking in the house I feel it going drop out of my hand and into one of those little cracks in the floor and disappear. So that's how I was walking with it cup in my hand and all the time I fretting that it sure to fall out. You notice how when a go to town where they have tile floor a still cup it but a never look down so much?…"

"So what happen now? You stop holding it?"

"Girl, is a long story. Suddenly one day the child change into one good-looking little boy with a square face and smooth smooth black skin… so bout two weeks a watching at my side to make sure he following me everywhere. Till one evening about three o'clock, I must be gazing, for you know B place strange, a just look round in time to see the little boy jump down inside a sink-hole… my heart leap, but you know, a didn't cry, is like I know that sink-hole didn't go to the sea. I follow my mind. Just as if somebody was guiding me. And a walk clear cross the town to where I think the sink-hole come out… I find the spot but not a sign of the child. Now you know how many years I been walking with that little one in my hand and a never had a mishap; and now this one, so much bigger, go lost from mi now. I sit down at the street side with me hand at mi chin. Then I walk back to where the sink-hole start, to see if it have another place where it come out again. But a find myself back to the same spot and a sit down again. This time I ready to cry. Dusk come, night start to fall. I sit down at the street side with my hand on my chin and somebody come up and pat me… Who you think? No the boy! Not a word… but with the matinee ticket in his hand… no show the boy go; and reach back safe and sound… I said "Jeezas Christ" and I look up to heaven but not a word mi no seh to him for afta we no talk.

"But from dat, I don't even look down to see if anybody nex to me and as you notice, is months now since I stop walk wid me han cup."

PARABLE III

You know that I can't swim. Not a stroke to save my life. But I love the water; like feel it pressing on my skin; like to pretend a going to push off forward and feel all my skin pressing against it.

Well this night I was pressing my body against this cool cool water. But it wasn't clear blue sea water; it was kinda blackish; like the water you get in the creeks in Guyana. And I was minding my business and thinking about God and about life how it great sometimes, when out of the corner of my eye I glimpse a hand stretching right up out of the water. I feel my heart stop. It wasn't any ordinary hand you know. It was a big big hand every finger almost the size of me. And the skin wasn't smooth. The hand make out of frog skin and it just stretching up there out of the water.

A trying to decide what to do and quickly start thinking about how to run. But my whole body was shivering and a suddenly realise that the water heavy. You ever try to run in the sea? Same time is as if a great mind read my thoughts and full up my head with the truth: the hand big, one finger as big as me; I can't swim; the water heavy and it wide. And the voice just speak inside me and say, "You too fool fool; go on and press you body 'gainst the water and enjoy youself. For if the hand come, it gwine catch you no matter what you do. And if it don't decide to come then you don't have no worries."

I look over the other side where a big white rock come up out of the water and a see a girl sitting on the rock holding a child on her knee. I don't know how a didn't notice her before; unless she wasn't there before. But a watch her and look at the baby and a notice even from that distance how the child favour my husband.

I just look away; and before a really think anything a find myself looking at the hand, the big frog-skin hand; and a feel a know something a didn't know before.

CAGES

"You beasts must love your cages after all…"
(Walcott, Joker of Seville)
?????? Joan, Jean, Joy

In the brown sofa, a geometrical figure, head lowered, trunk resting on a triangle of thighs and legs, Hugh sits. Joan passes the cup and seats herself in the couch opposite. The fragrance of Blue Mountain coffee clouds them slow, invisibly. Hugh, with great deliberateness, raises his head, waits, lowers it, and takes a quick, hot sip. Joan suddenly finds herself staring, contemplating a huge, brooding, oversized bird; caught in a cage.

In the zoo, animals have enough space for the occasional short exploratory sally. A bird of Hugh's size would have a very large cage with enough space for a good whirl now and then. And even so they show claustrophobic tendencies.

"I want to talk to you."

"About what?"

"The marriage and everything."

"What about them?"

"How me and you not communicating at all."

"What you mean not communicating? I find we communicating quite well."

"I don't mean like that. I mean we not feeling comfortable and happy in the relationship with each other and I don't even feel sure you want me around."

This wasn't going very well. It sounded surprisingly like several earlier attempts on the same subject. The tone of response was the same too, gruff and impatient. This pause was too long; sort of ominous.

"What you want me to do now, tell you a love you and things like that?"

"I don't want you to lie to me and tell me things you don't mean."

"Is what you want then, woman? Listen, all I want now is to read this book and to be able to read it by myself. That is why I came out here in the first place. You ever hear about people needing to be alone? Well that is what I need right now. A person can't even sit down a little by themself without you coming with you stupid paranoia. You half-crazy noh, but you not going send me off my head too."

Put like that, it all sounded very reasonable. Joan started to wonder whether she did, as Hugh frequently suggested, make her own problems then start to worry about them. Maybe she was complicating this marriage by her anxiety; she so desperately wanted it to go well. But could it really be so unfair to expect Hugh even just to talk to her sometimes? – in more than monosyllables, that is.

★

Joan lay in bed and moved out of the flat in a reverie that threatened to become obsessive. She must run away; leave Hugh and give him a chance; give herself a chance. They were destroying each other. He said he was okay but he probably just didn't want to think about it. She certainly wasn't. There had to be more than that to life. These days she found herself talking to herself after the older children had left for school. Nowhere had she read about or imagined such loneliness. Married loneliness… call it what you will. You communicate all day with small children; you find yourself living for the evening and adult companionship and when it comes… it wants to be alone.

Hugh said she was like an octopus trying to hold him in a sort of multiple embrace. That sounded truly original and perhaps it was… great minds? Anyway she had noted the same image in a psychology book for laymen. Perhaps he even read psychology books on the sly all the while swearing they were confusing her brain:

"Listen, no two people alike; no two couples alike. How anybody can tell you how to fix yourself just because they fix some other people completely different from you… only a clown like you could swallow so much stupidness." She didn't want to own Hugh, or anything like that. She just wanted him to recognise the hand behind the coffee cup – sometimes. The thing with marriage is that it takes you out of your own little circle of girls and fellows then offers you nothing in exchange. And the man who spent so much time trying to be with you suddenly finds every ruse to be without you or starts looking very pained if he has to be with you.

But she had tried to make it bearable. Take the time Shadwell used to come by Sunday nights and bring his records so they could listen – he to hers, she to his – to such a fine selection between them… Hugh never liked her kind of music. Too melodramatic he used to say; those fantastic horns! So he would drift away to the bedroom. You can't expect to share all the same interests yourself and your husband, so a guileless, young, sensible chap like Shads – where is the harm in that? But one Sunday night he was a little late and Hugh said in his deadpan voice:

"What happen, you boyfriend not coming tonight?"

And you know that throw such a damper on the whole thing that she start to show the young man bad face… Amen to that. You either make a big fuss and a big point over a small thing like that, or forget it.

Or take the time she asked him whether she could invite Peter, the nice new fellow on the staff, over to the house so he could meet him:

"As long as when I bring any girls in here you don't mind." She hadn't meant it that way and Hugh knew that. So she never invited Peter though he collected blown-glass pieces too and wanted to see her collection. Of course when he decided that girls was the thing, he went for them with a zest she hadn't seen him display about anything since he stopped stoning mangoes.

"You not sleeping?"

"Mmmmmm."

"What you setting up for without even a book in you hand?"

"I was just thinking…"

"I don't want to hear what you thinking. Every day for the past six years you been thinking the same thing. I want to sleep. You better try a little of that too."

In no time she was listening to him snore… curled up; his back a smooth curve, his knees forming an angle with his nose; accommodating his body, even in that peculiar shape, to the narrowness of the bed. Gathering the blanket about her, Joan settled into her small cage and concentrated on the shaft of light coming in through a peephole from the street outside. She knew she had found no answers.

CAGE II

"I didn't want to tell you on the telephone."

"What? I can't hear you."

"I say I didn't want to tell you on the telephone."

"Didn't want to tell me what?"

"I'm not coming on Tuesday."

"What's happening, can't you get a flight?"

"I'm not coming back at all!"

"What?"

"I say I'm not coming back; I've found somebody else!"

"Somebody else?"

"Yes, but you don't know him! – Hello! Hello! Hello! Jim, are you there?"

Jim's mouth hung open. His hand held the phone limply as if he would drop it any minute. The blood coloured his face right up to the roots of his sparse straight hairs. With much clattering of plastic, he replaced the phone on its hook, stuck his hands deep in his pockets and walked out the door leaving it wide open.

It was difficult, almost impossible for him to imagine Jean with somebody else, smiling at him, dancing with him, making… no, she couldn't possibly make love to him. She had said he didn't know him so the obvious questions presented themselves: good-looking? rich? foreign? But how could all this matter. What must he have to offer to let her risk the marriage? He must be very rich. Perhaps that was a little unfair. She never was a great one for money. In any case he had given her everything she ever asked for. Look at their home, so elegant! The children so pretty and well behaved. And of course himself, a professional man of some standing. He had worked long and hard to deserve the Duke Street shingle and now the practice was thriving…

"John, my wife has left me!"

"Eh?"

"She's left me. She found another man!"

"Jeff, my wife has left me."

"She's left me. She found another man!"

"Jerry, my wife has left me!"

"Eh?"

"She's left me. She found another man!"

"Come Jim."

"Yes Jim."

"Yes man."

"Let's have a drink then we can talk about it."

"Jean."

"Yes Mummy."

"You thought about it? You sure you doing the right thing?"

"Jean."

"Yes Joan."

"You thought about it? You sure you doing the right thing?"

"Jean."

"Yes Aileen."

"You thought about it? You sure you doing the right thing?"

"What about the children?"

The children?"

"The children?"

"You remember when we were little we used to play in that cave called Daddy Rock and jump to catch the little rock fingers hanging from the roof? Well, imagine a large stone at the cave mouth and imagine yourself inside with the children and the washing and the cooking; and the original caveman coming home every night and moving the stone a little so you just glimpse the light of day and grunting and getting into bed or grunting, changing and leaving again, putting the stone back into place! Now watch that three hundred and sixty-five times multiplied by five!

"The children? When he's at home he's asleep or they are asleep. Sometimes he takes them out of course, but that's so rare. His life is full and complicated. His clients are demanding. He can't find time to share things with the family. Tell me I sound melodramatic but I haven't lived for five years. I had forgotten even how to dream, for every dream was a nightmare. I had to come here, and get the picture from a distance; and now I can't go back.

"No, don't blame Charles, he just happened along when I most needed someone. I didn't know how bad the living was. Thirty years old is not the end of the line. You know I may even have thirty left! Jim always told me I was so old!"

"But now Charles says he wants to marry you! He told your father that last night."

"He'll get over it. Not me again. Once bitten…

"Listen Mummy, I have a feeling this generation of men and women can't make it. We are caught in a funny in-between something. But don't worry. The next generation will. This generation of women asking for bread and the men offering them crumbs. Now we can feed, house, clothe ourselves, we looking for something more. And most of them never learned to take the trouble. You know I have been talking to Charles every night for three weeks now. And I don't think it's just because he's a new friend, for I'm not telling him my life history. It's just plain starvation for adult company. And if he were my husband, ten chances to one he wouldn't want to talk to me. I wonder what is in marriage now for 'inside women'. 'Honorary wives'?"

I'm glad I told him. I feel like a great weight has fallen from my shoulders. I feel light. A bird, suddenly, without a cage.

CAGE III

Casual and clean, Hugh with his slow smile looks past the open door to the table covered with file paper:

"What you working on?"

"Nothing much."

"Don't let me interrupt you."

"It's okay. Sit down."

Noiselessly, like a cat, Joy moves over to the chair facing him, forgetting her papers. He, absorbing her peace and her quiet, admires her legs, diminutive, shapely, smooth and unblemished below the red shorts; curled up, he thinks, like a contented cat.

"Cigarettes?"

"Thanks. I won't open my pack then."

She throws the matches; two paces slowly and he lights hers then his, resettles himself in the sofa and puffs off, exhaling the smoke into her silence.

"Finished your packing?"

"Nothing much to pack."

"What time tomorrow?"

"Tell them six, sevenish; okay, six-thirty."

"I asked Miss Ruby to open the flat from early morning so it will be fresh."

"Thanks. Is there anything you don't think of?"

Ask my wife, he thought; she will give you a list. But he only smiled his shy half-smile into her silence.

"Have a drink."

"Yes, christen the place."

"What?"

"Christen the flat."

"Blasphemer."

"No man, we say that here."

29

"Okay, cheers."

Scotch and ginger, weak, she had poured. Women are really peculiar the kinds of things they remember… slowly stirring the drink with his finger.

"This place look like you already."

"How?"

"Small and neat; everything just right."

"Thanks. And by the way, thanks for the flowers too; notice where I put them? Centre forward. Cigarette?"

"Thanks. You never smoke anything but Anchor?"

"Only if I can't get…"

"Not complaining. Suits me fine."

A quiet drink and a quiet smoke. Hugh could feel his body recharging itself slowly but surely, restoring the tissues worn by the demands of the office, by the wordless demands of his institutionalised wife over dinner, by the chorus of needs of the children afterwards.

"Busy tomorrow?"

"What, Saturday? No."

"Pick you up after lunch then?"

"Make it two; after my after-lunch sleep; any place special?"

"Your wish my love; my beautiful new engine –"

"Bring the map with you," and she smiles her small even teeth to him and gazes at him from under the lids of her wahly cat eyes.

And so the ritual goes. Hugh protecting, taking care like nobody before, except Grandma. Grandma protecting a child's slightness with her age and authority; correcting without reproach, scolding with obvious love:

"Keep you hat on, Copper-rat; you hair soon get red like you face," grabbing the straw hat with its floppy brim and pressing it firmly on an unsteady head, tugging the sides to keep it well on. Grandma who thought her daughter owed her one of the children at least; and that had to be her obvious favourite. No diplomat was Grandma; she wanted Copper-rat, frail, "she needs looking after" and "light-skinned like her father". And the legs Hugh was for ever complimenting, he should thank her:

"Copper, here's a new pair of jeans for you. Don't let me catch you playing in the grass without them. You will mark up you pretty skin." Gran couldn't have taken the same trouble with her own children for their skin was full of blemishes; especially the girls... Perhaps she just didn't have the time then, too much to do.

Much later there had been Marshall; but he never heard about taking care of; taken care of perhaps. Love, yes; a whole lot of passion; violent sometimes and unpredictable... today, yes, tomorrow, no... that for years then suddenly, nothing!

This with Hugh is much calmer, a sort of low, constant flow, like a pilot light? Hugh a pilot? Big hulking pilot but gentle and compassionate...

"A penny for your..."

"No, you can't buy them." He could barely see the edges of her teeth again.

"Why?"

"Too personal and too ancient."

"Come off it. I'm the ancient one around here."

"What about a show tonight?"

"Anything good on?"

"Moulin Rouge. Saw it already?"

"Yes, years and years ago, but it can take a second."

"Okay, we have an hour or so."

At the office the fellows didn't like it; cramp their style.

"Joy –"

"Yes –"

"So when we having this drink at Mountain?"

"Which drink?"

"You know well –"

"Why you asking when you know Hugh don't want me to go?"

"Girl, you don't see this married man lock you up in a cage? You in one and his wife in another; two of you can't even be on the street the same night!"

"Lucian, I will ask you advice when I want it."

"Okay, Mam, apologies. But if you ever decide to fly out of the cage, give me a shout..."

Perhaps when the door is open, you can't really feel the cageness of the cage.

TALES OF MOTHERING

Sister I

Manhattan. The morning was quiet, cool and sharp with the crisp of April.

The white Upper East Side – rich, white Anglo-Saxon ghetto – rose slowly, throwing off its filmy dressing-gowns and pulling languid drapes admitting (at ten am) the light of another day. Park Avenue, the lot that worked, took Danish and coffee. Jewish ex-women, now park mothers, watched their offspring play and set their minds to sharing foolish chatter… and could not feel their own incipient madness…

Ten o'clock chimed from the chapel clock in the holy school-yard. The taximan on the corner, obedient to the light, stopped and saw… Swift through the air, cutting the nothing like white light, a flash of packaged debris; packaged white… one, two, three… in arcs from a balcony on the high apartment building. But no one moved.

In New York, there are older women, in orange overalls or blue, to help at traffic crossings so the tiniest child can reach the pavement and walking on it find, eventually, home. And when school people take the small ones to the park to do their sandbox and their climbing things, women must cross with them, one woman and a hundred tiny feet behind.

The old lady, banner forward, forcing the traffic to a halt, approached the corner and suddenly with one hurried right-hand motion checked the concourse of tiny feet, the rush of tiny eyes. She saw no arcs of light. She saw no garbage packaged white but children's twisted faces one and two and the agonised stare in a young woman's face and all three bodies showing broken on the pavement. With both hands now she checked the concourse, turned the phalanx back. "Holy Mary Mother of God," the old woman crossed herself.

Manhattan. The morning became loud; the noise of sirens rushing through the street. Somebody must have phoned. Police, ambulance; Manhattan matrons rising late wrinkled their foreheads in why and later wondered loudly why the blacks can't keep their messy business far uptown. It's all our fault, they say, just fancy, blacks in Upper white East Side…

At the UN ladies' once-per-month tea, faces of all shades and patterns turned to a screen of slides at the far end of the room. The voice of the translator intoned… "My village is a hundred kilometres from the capital…" A tall elegant woman speaks the next line in French and changes the slide. Yards and yards of intricate tie-dye in gorgeous colours sheathe her. Later, women with impossible names speaking impossible languages eat savoury West African pastry. It is Senegal this month; next month it is China and amid the din of voices this tete-a-tete:

"I feel so bad about it."

"It hurt me up man."

"You can imagine how I feel? I live in the building, you know."

"You know her well then?"

"No. That's why I feel so bad. You know how many times I make to talk to her in the elevator? But you know how foolish you feel making conversation with all those white people staring silent? And besides with my few words of French and she don't know English…"

"But even if you didn't talk to her maybe somebody else did –"

"Not a chance. Most probably not a soul. You can imagine the loneliness she was in to make her do a thing like that? She was young, you know, about twenty-five with those two little children. The husband is a dresser. You don't know him? Dress sharp every morning and gone; and you know those committees sometimes go on into night –"

"I wonder how him feel?"

"Tell you the truth my mind too full of her to think about him."

36

Sister II

"She left, that's what she did."

"But how? And when? Everything seemed so happy… then!"

"Yes, yes, but she is gone. I very busy this last week, come back from meeting, find her gone… that's all."

"But where? Any idea where?"

"How must I know? She took taxi; took money, passport. I think she went on plane –"

I didn't try to speak. I couldn't. Too shocked. Too struck with marvelling at this little girl, my daughter almost, hardly twenty… to plot and plan in such short time to fly from Georgetown to Mali?

"He prays too much," she had said. "He's old; he has to pray. He near to die. Me young. Me not pray so much." And later, very solemn now, "Marriage is hard. I miss my family. I miss my books… and all this English!…"

"I give her house. I give her food. Music and English lessons. What more she want?" (My colleague was getting angry now; indignant.) "I write her parents right away."

I looked at him and wondered what parents, religious custom, what harsh rule could tie a young girl to an educated stud. He was high, she had said. High in religion and in politics; and city. She was from a country town. I never asked her any more.

I stared at him and threw my hands in helpless empathising gesture at this timeless man. That story I had heard before… without this end… I laughed inside. This end was fine indeed. The young today are not so young. This was no time to grieve…

II: MY MOTHER
For Marjorie

The Lexington Avenue train raced into Fourteenth Street station like a runaway horse and miraculously came to a stop; belching forth such an army of fast-moving bodies that I flattened myself against the stair-rails in sheer terror. But I survived, and after the first flight of stairs, stood near a tiny candyshop in the station, to let them all pass.

I stared, but only at the blacks – the strangers whom this heartless machine had rushed out of Harlem, out of the safety of the familiar 125th Street and into this alien city; to dingy stores and tiny disorganised offices or to other vague connections: Canarsie, Long Island, Jamaica, etc. They were all running, in some way or other – in careless abandon or in crisp, short, overbred paces; the women's girdles and eventually their coats, controlling the obviousness of the movement; the men's coat-tails flapping at the inevitable slit below the rump.

The men, whether they were briefcase types or lunch-pan types, all wore little hats with short brims. It was a cold morning. In New York twenty-three degrees is considered cold. The women didn't need hats. Cheap, curly wigs hugged their temples protecting their black youthfulness and hiding their kinky strands. Fifty acknowledging thirty needs a wig. For some reason the real hairline tells a story even when it is dyed black. And here the merciful cold allowed for the constant sweater or the little scarf that covers the telltale neck.

Everybody was running and everybody looked frightened. But you could see that all this had become natural. This speed was now normal and because they couldn't see their own frightened faces, they couldn't recognise their fright. When you answer long enough to a name that for one reason or another is wrong, and when you live long enough with a face that is always wrong, a frightened look grows on you and becomes an inseparable part of you. I looked at them and became numb with a kind of nameless grief. For I had seen my mother for the first time in all those tense women's faces, in all those heads hiding their age and gentleness beneath the black, curly wigs.

The little journey was a ritual. Very early, the first or second Saturday morning of the month, my grandmother and I would walk to Anne's Ridge and get in the line at the bank. I would sign my name on the money order made out to me and we would soon move from the Foreign Exchange line to the Savings line. I never knew how much money came, for the exchange from dollars to pounds was too much for me to handle, and I never knew how much was saved. But I always felt, one Saturday every month, that we were rich.

Sometimes we stopped in the big Anne's Ridge stores in town and bought a new plate or two, sometimes dress material and, v-e-r-y occasionally, shoes. Then we stopped in the market for the few things Gran didn't plant and Mass Nathan's shop didn't stock.

The journey home was less pleasant. I never ever noticed the hills on the way back, not because they were so much less green but because it took all my energy to think up little stories to help me block out Gran's monthly lecture. It always had to do with ingratitude. I'm not sure now how she knew the extent of my ingratitude long before I even understood the concept of gratitude. It had to do with the faithfulness of her daughter working hard in America to support me so I could "come to something" and my not trying to show thanks. I was no great writer, but Gran saw to it that I scratched something on an airletter form to my mother every month and that something always included thanks for the money.

Gran never made it clear in what nonverbal ways I should express thanks. I had to do well at school; but the teachers had a sort of foolproof mechanism for assuring that – those were the days of the rod and I meant to be a poor customer for that. So school was okay. But the guidelines at home were less clear. An action that one day was a sign of ingratitude was, next day, a normal action. It seems that the assessment of my behaviour was a very arbitrary and subjective exercise and depended partly on Gran's moods.

Now I understand what Gran's dilemma was like. She herself did not know what she had to produce from the raw material she was given if her daughter's sacrifice was not to be meaningless. She had been set a great task and she was going to acquit herself manfully at all costs, but she was swimming in very strange waters. Her daughter could only work and send money, and she couldn't offer guidelines either – only vague hints like the necessity for me to speak properly, however that should be.

Every year we expected my mother home on vacation and every year she wrote that she was sorry she couldn't make it. But she always sent, as if to represent her, a large round box that people insisted on calling a barrel. It was full of used clothes of all sorts, obviously chosen with little regard for my size or my grandmother's size. I never went to the collecting ceremony. This involved a trip to Kingston and endless red-tape. I merely waited at the gate till the bus turned the curve, gave its two honks and slid along the loose stones to a halt to let my grandmother out. Then the sideman would roll the barrel along the top of the bus and shove it to his comrade. Immediately the bus would honk again and move on.

Nothing smells exactly like my mother's boxes. It was a smell compounded from sweat and mustiness and black poverty inheriting white castoffs. I still remember one of those dresses from the box. With today's eyes I can see that it was a woman's frock, a short woman's voile frock for cocktail parties or an important lunch. And I was nine or ten then. But I wore it with pride, first to the Sunday School Christmas concert and then to numerous "social" events thereafter. And even now, that low-slung waist or anything resting lightly on the hips has particular charm for me, whether or not the beholder's eye shares my judgement… There were blouses and shoes and hats; something to fit almost everyone in my grandmother's endless chronicle of cousins. We accepted our ill-fitting fits and wore them with surprising confidence.

Every year we expected my mother home on vacation. But she never came. The year I was in third form they flew her body home. I hadn't heard that she was ill. I felt for months afterwards that my very last letter should have said something different, something more, should have shown more gratitude than the others. But I could not possibly have known that that would be the last.

When the coffin arrived it was clear that nobody from Jamaica had touched that coffin. Sam Isaacs may have kept it a few days but that was all. The whole thing was foreign – large, heavy, silvery – straight from the USA. And when they opened the lid in the church, so she could lie in state and everybody could look and cry, it was clear that my mother too had been untouched by local hands. She had come straight from the USA.

When my mother left Jamaica I couldn't have been more than five or six, so any memory I had of her was either very vague or very clear and original – carved out of my own imagination with patterns all mixed up, of other people's mothers and of those impersonal clothes in the annual barrel. The woman in the coffin was not my mother. The woman in the purple dress and black shoes (I didn't even know they buried people in shoes), the highly powdered face, framed by jet-black curls and covered lightly with a mantilla, was not like any of the several images I had traced.

The funeral couldn't be our funeral. It was a spectacle. I don't suppose more than half the people there had actually known my mother. But it was a Sunday, and the whole week that had elapsed between the news of her death and the actual funeral made it possible for people from far and near to make the trip to our village. Those who were from surrounding districts but had jobs in the city used one stone to kill two birds – visit the old folks at home, and come up to "Miss Angie daughter funeral".

It wasn't our funeral. It was a spectacle.

The afternoon was hot; inside the church was hotter. Outside, I stood as far as I could from the grave and watched several of them pointing at me, their eyes full of tears: "Dats de little wan she lef wid Miss Angie." Near to me was a woman in a fur hat, close fitting, with a ribbon at the side. She wore a dress of the same yellow gold as the hat, long earrings and costume jewellery of the same yellow gold.

41

I could hear the trembling voices from the grave –

> "I know not oh I know not
> What joys await me there…"

– and fur hat, beside me, trying to outdo them so her friend could hear her:

"A didn know ar but a sih dih face; is fat kill ar noh?" (My mother was rather busty but that was as far as the fat went).

She didn't wait for an answer but continued: "A nevva sih wan of dese deds that come back from England yet." (No one had taken the trouble to tell her it was America not England.)

"But de reason why a come to see ar is becaaz I was dere meself an a always seh ef a ded, dey mus sen mih back. Is now a sih ow a woulda look! But tengad a lucky a come back pon me own steam… An you sih dis big finneral shi have? She wouldn't have get it in Englan' you know. Since one o'clock she woulda gaan an' if they cremate ar, while we drinking a cuppa tea, she bunnin'."

"Wat?" asked her audience at last. "Deh gives tea? An peeple siddung?"

"Man, deh put dem in someting like ovin, an by dih time we jus' drink dih tea, you get dih ashes an' you gaan."

They had stopped singing about my mother's joys; the slow heavy dirge was now "Abide with me", sung with the Baptist rhythm sad and slow, though I hardly think it is possible for that particular song to be anything but sad and slow, Baptist or no Baptist. I looked towards the crowd. They were supporting my grandmother. I knew she wasn't screaming. She was never given to screaming. She was just shaking as great sobs shook her body and her hands seemed to hold up her stomach. It was pointless my trying to comfort her; they wouldn't let me. Two old women were holding her, Miss Emma, her good friend, and Cousin Jean, who was more like a sister than a cousin.

Next day I went alone to my mother's grave to push my own little bottle with maidenhair fern into the soft, red earth. When all their great wreaths with purple American ribbons had long faded, my maidenhair fern started to grow.

I had never known my mother. I had known her money and

her barrels and my grandmother's respect for her. I had not wept at her funeral. But that morning, in the subway station at Fourteenth Street, in the middle of nowhere, in the midst of a certain timelessness, I wept for her, unashamedly, and for the peace at Anne's Ridge that she never came back to know, after the constant madness, after the constant terror of all the Fourteenth Street subway stations in that horrifying workhouse.

I saw my tears water the maidenhair fern on her grave to a lush green luxuriance. I was glad I was a guest in the great USA and a guest didn't need a wig. I would take no barrels home with me. I saw my mother's ancient grave covered again with its large and gaudy wreaths. Like the mad old man in Brooklyn, I lifted from a hundred imaginary heads a hundred black and curly wigs and laid them all on the ancient grave. And I laid with them all the last shapeless, ill-fitting clothes from the last barrel. The last of the women had hurried away. I wept for my mother. But I rejoiced that the maidenhair fern was lush and that we had no longer need for gaudy wreaths.

III: GRAN...
Portrait of one kind of woman

When we were little, remember, the world was full of pastures and pastures were full of cow-dung. Everybody's farm had its own little pasture which everybody else used as a short-cut to get from one field to another, or from one yard to another, or from either to the main road. And every morning each pasture seemed to have as many hot new loads of dung as it had cows; and every morning flies crowded anxiously around each hot new load. Everyone knew that if you were ill-mannered and tried to pass the flies unnoticed, they all rose up at you and pitched mercilessly in your eyes, on your nose and even on your lips; but if you greeted them as you passed they left you alone. And so we went our way through pasture to school, or shop or neighbour's house and slowed down near each load murmuring, "Good morning, good morning, good morning."

The oven-house was no longer empty. Swarthy old women, each with her long hair in a single braid, squatted near the ground each with her long skirt completely shrouding her legs and emphasising tiny hillocks that were withered knees. There was a look at once vacuous and resigned on each face and each slack mouth drooped as if all elasticity had left it. The white marl floor had somehow disappeared or was completely covered with cane-trash obviously brought from the boiling-house in that dim, all-but-forgotten past and since traversed a thousand times by hurried feet; now no more than black powder more suitable for plant manure than floor. There were flies all over the floor, merging with the blackened cane dust, or rising a mere three inches from the ground in swarms, to get an aerial view of their comrades. I knew that saying good morning to these flies couldn't achieve anything, for they were not really rising up at me; it was only that when in the normal run of their business they rose for the routine aerial view, they brushed endlessly about my feet, never breaking off for a moment their cruel unending zing zong.

I don't know how I had passed it all to reach the far side of this dingy little plaza, but I must have, for soon I was leaning on the old oven itself. The brick I was resting on shook with my every breath and yielded patches of yellow dust from its little volcano. I felt an urgent desire to get back to the entrance, to find some retreat from the rotting place, so I started to cross the courtyard. I looked down to choose my steps and noticed only then that my feet were bare. And the powdered cane-trash became dried filth, and my toes felt as if they would unhinge themselves and I knew that no amount of washing could ever make my feet clean again. But I walked on through the inexorable filth and while each step was still incomplete, a swarm of flies, anticipating the next foothold, would rise with their buzzing; and a new panic would seize me, a new urgency to hasten the painfully slow journey. The women were all creasing their foreheads, flat like dingy squares of off-white sugar paper; they were all gazing at the ground and moaning, "Craab, craab, craab." And I couldn't figure out then whether crab meant filth or flies or whether it was some ancient expression of pity.

In an eternity I had reached the entrance and heard a solemn voice, "…but I had warned you not to come," and I felt that there was wonder on my face and terror; wonder that couldn't fathom how that scene that I had longed for all these years had come with time to this. Change, yes, I had heard of it, and understood in terms on cold paper what had taken place, but face to face with truth… fiction could never be a patch upon fact.

"Craab, craab, craab," the old women continued to whine, and suddenly it all made sense. Back there in the time of good morning to flies, Landcrab had been a symbol of cleanliness. His legs would fall off if he ever touched filth, they said. So it was my feet. They were mocking the scorn they could sense on my feet for their floor; the floor on which their circumstance forced them to squat day-in, day-out. It wasn't pity then, or anything like it. It was their particular brand of sarcasm. Then the scorn and the terror fell at once from me, and in their place another kind of scorn; for myself, for the monster of insensitivity who couldn't control my response, who couldn't find out how in one automatic reaction to protect my psyche and their sensitivity. Reality makes such a mess of things; one man's meat is another man's poison; Gopaul luck a noh Seepaul luck. Even natural things like germs take sides. I would surely get sick if I stuck around there, there in the place that for these shrivelled old women was home.

Beyond the entrance, there was the space the house used to occupy. But there was nothing there to remind me even dimly of a house. Not even the usual telltale patch of extra greenness on the brown/green earth. The whole structure had long crumbled and I could see with my mind's eye people passing through the yard in any of four directions along the paths which, running parallel to certain main roads, always proved to be shorter and more private, and removing, one or two at a time, any boards that still had use in them.

My aunt had hoped for a hospital here; she couldn't ever picture this... but the money she sent, a fortune to her, was a mere pittance; and while the government made up its red-tape mind, these poor souls must have moved in one by one... but from where? Which place could have been poor enough to have anybody move from there to this? Perhaps the house had been here when they came... but old and falling apart; and when the kitchen survived it, they moved there... and sleep now on any number of rags... old rags... and lounge in the daytime in this oven-house, cooking in the old oven zally, or sometimes on a naked fire outside where I could see the three stones, blackened, and the ashes... cooking always bananas from the trees behind the kitchen; always small now, stunted and diseased as succeeding generations of bananas will always get without fertiliser, without agricultural instructors' advice and without care. Some fruit trees were okay though, like the naseberries, so they eat those when they bear and besides, I hear they take turns at begging in the district come Sunday morning...

The kitchen used to be large, remember. Breakfast there was sitting on a long bench on the far side of the fire. Granny never trusted us near. And Gran herself, passing the chocolate, piping hot in the tin cans with handles akimbo, *be careful*, and the ruuti and saltfish fried and floating in oil, fresh home-made coconut oil with skellion and black pepper inside. Sounds so large now, more like lunch, but we would be hungry again in an hour or two… all play and no work…

I set the tin of biscuits down and tried not to stare – for they were smiling now, creasing not only foreheads but cheeks as well – and started down the hill. But I looked back as Lot's wife did and froze into my mind a new last picture of Comfort Hall. It was no longer Gran, clean, beautiful, but senile and lonely, but five pale old women, risen from their dust, inching their way at their maximum speed towards the biscuit tin I had left. The youngest of them and tallest too, or perhaps merely less bent, while the others smiled and waved their bony hands, was opening the tin with clawlike fingers, her body arching over it like a parson John Crow saying his "Shwaa, shwaa" before a bone-cleaning ceremony…

"Wat kill im?"

"Fat kill im."

"Whose iz di baddy?"

"Yourrrrrz."

Halfway down the pass I sat on the bank covered with silence. The grass was still damp with last night's dew. I looked out in a straight line and saw the silent sun rising on to the hill and on to the church with its brown steeple growing out of the hill. The school was there too, no longer new as it was when we sat on bamboo benches and shivered as teacher traced our line of knees with the guava whip…

I lit a cigarette and immediately remembered how Gran would have objected. She didn't like shaved armpits in a woman either, or whistling, or any number of actions she considered unnatural. You had to keep the list open for minor additions as each situation revealed a new one. I was staring at the steeple and thinking that I shouldn't have come. I should have kept my images right down to the last guilt-ridden encounter that would never now be last again. These shrivelled old women, ugly in all their dirt and deprivation, the lacklustre leaves and dying vegetation, could never be Comfort Hall. Memory knew lush landscape, healthy fruit and Gran in all her different faces.

The old women there on the hill were only good to prove to all those half-baked philosophers shouting optimism that there is nothing so great about tomorrow or about today for that matter. Comfort Hall had somehow joined Greece and Rome and Ozymandias' works. After this it would be difficult to see the past with any honesty or truth. Everything would wear a halo now for it had to be compared with those old women and their vomit-pulling filth.

The sun, competing against itself, had risen steadily and blazed now on the bank and through the leaves of the tangerine tree. The leaves looked smaller than I remembered them; like the bananas; perhaps like most things there on the land if you took the trouble to look; all suffering the same kraurosis, the same menopausal atrophy; suffering and exposed to the merciless eye of this microscoping morning.

Children, children
  Yes Mummah
Where have you been to?
  Grand-mummah
What did she give you?
  Bread and Pear…

If you thought of yourself in relation to the "V" in the tangerine tree, you could see time rushing past your eyes like the landscape through a speeding bus window. It wasn't so long ago, or was it? you could stand in that very "V" and rest, and then ascend with two vast lunges forward, to a point from which you could pull in the laden branch and sit and quietly gorge yourself on as many yellow, soft-skinned fruit as you could take. Tangerines were endlessly fascinating. Some of them had babies, not all, and you couldn't really tell from the outside whether they had; if there was a navel at the base you thought yes, but this test failed so often it was like a rule of grammar or, of course, it was the rule of life: not all women have babies. The baby was exactly like the mother, whenever you found one, same shape, same colour, but sweeter when you tasted it, and of course much smaller. After the baby, you attacked the mother, and after six tangerines or so, when the edge of hunger was off and it was no longer necessary to shove four pegs into your mouth at a time, you started to enjoy the aesthetics of the tangerine. So now you stripped each peg of its white, antimacassar decoration patiently (you even remembered that if you swallowed that you could get appendicitis); you looked at the occasional peg in detail, always on the point of bursting but always managing to control that, as each beautiful turgid cell inside pressed against the transparent womb-wall. No matter how carefully you bit it, it would spill, spraying yellow juice all over your play clothes or your good

49

clothes, depending on your luck, as if in one bite you had decapitated not one but at least a dozen juice-filled cells. A tangerine: a sort of triple womb, juice living in hundreds of tiny cells protected by their own cell walls, sitting together in a fruit-tissue womb, pegs sitting side by side in a heavy yellow rind womb. Nature is birth repeated a hundred times over.

The tangerine tree sent a slim but sturdy smooth limb to hang out over the pass. It was smooth with the smoothness of many hands; no one could resist it. As you came up the pass you felt compelled to swing with your right hand on that overhanging bough, and now after so many years it was still smooth; a human hand would have become gnarled by now... How many people still used that pass? How many people now swing with their right hand on that bough? Perhaps the smoothness of the limb did not depend on today's or yesterday's hands. Perhaps nothing can undo what years of palm sweat and pressure had done so long ago. For the limb had always been an important point on the journey uphill... hanging there at right angles to the garden and a few steps from the concrete barbecue. It was from there that you announced yourself after the long trek up the hill. It was close enough for anyone in the house or even in the kitchen to hear you... just barely... If you were a child hoping for a fruit or some bake-bake, a toto or a gizada or a bullah cake, then you started your "Mawnin Madda" right there, being careful to let your voice rise steadily to a crescendo on the second syllable of the "Madda". But you never picked a tangerine if you were a stranger. Miss Eva had given the world strict orders not to touch her fruit; the world that is, excluding her precious grandchildren who, whenever they were around, had all kinds of unreasonable rights. You would resist the temptation to pick a tangerine and chance your fortune on whatever your greeting gave her time to find.

"Morning little chicken" – that after your second or third signal from the tangerine tree, all the time swinging your palm on the overhanging branch.

"Who is that?"

"Meery, Mam."

"Come Meery, take this for your mother."

That was always a good sign for it would be impossible for

Miss Eva to send something for your mother without giving you something for yourself, so you anticipated the next sentence:

"– And this for you and the others."

"This" may be more tangerines than you could possibly have stolen had you tried, or a bag of star-apples, or of course some baked things ready to eat. Miss Eva never gave any indication of the ratio in which you should divide it between yourself and the others, but anyone with a grain of sense and a drop of self-love knew exactly how to share it and, what is more, knew how to start unwrapping the parcel and eat a few first helpings when the last shingle of Miss Eva's kitchen disappeared.

It was here at the same tangerine tree that we, the precious grandchildren, would rest our suitcase on the ground, take one swing and shout:

"Graneeeeeeeeeeee!" And if she failed to hear that first cry we would parody a district child and sing:

"Evenin Madaaaaaah!" but she would invariably catch the voice and banter back:

"Don't call mi Madda, Madda walk wid stick –"

And with that she would dash from the kitchen as agile as a rabbit, through the oven-house and across the gravel, making music as she grazed it with her heavy coarse boots. She would hug you welcome and wipe her hands in her apron so that you were never sure where one action stopped and the other began. In those days she was ageless.

She said sixty but we couldn't believe so many years behind that face. The smell of tomorrow's buns enveloped you with that hug; a smell that perfumed her calico apron permanently. The apron itself was quite extraordinary. It was bound twice round her slim waist and was more like a wrap skirt than an apron. Of course there was skirt under it, though only the texture of the material labelled one skirt and the other apron. Under that was a petticoat. All this meant that Gran's hug was extremely soft. You felt however that there was definitely some superfluity of garments there. Why petticoat when she wore a slip? But that was like asking why flannel when there was slip-bodice? And the answer to that was that young people like your mother would all die of pneumonia because they didn't wear enough clothes.

We heard that Gran had been tough in her time. Heard that from our parents, that generation. But none of the toughness belonged to our time. We were phase two, always more gentle than phase one (second wives and grandchildren are the envy of first wives and children). To us she was indulgent, loving and lyrical, and in complete command of all baked food, all fruits of the earth and even of God.

Cold Comfort Hall mornings; bleary-eyed ten-year-old indolence; Gran up with the first crow of morning:

> "Get up little chickens
> Rise up betimes
> Go forth alone
> Because thy God is near! …"

And so in a rush, small feet down the hill for buckets of water; watch or the slope sends bucket and owner cascading dizzy down to the yam fields below. Don't forget to stop where the coco leaves grow thickest and wash those dull eyes with chilly dew water; good for your eyes you won't need glasses later. Single-file up the hill, bare black legs making everlasting angles with the red hillside slope.

Buckets carefully balanced; put a big coco leaf on top so the water keeps steady or your head or your dress will be wet without mercy. Finish your four trips by the time the sun lifts the mist from the valley, displacing it inch by inch and reaching the hilltop.

Bath; breakfast; work.

Gran baking thousands of buns and totos and grattos (supermarkets now stock this as a piece of exotica labelled "grotto"), that superb triangular bread-flap. Involving me totally in the business of baking; offering me apron and portion of bun dough; then her face gleaming with pleasure as my minuscule replicas of her own buns took their places neat near her elegant buns in their "laatas"; my biscuit-tin-top containers like lowly third cousins. Out in the sun as her large buns rose, so the third cousins rose in their midget containers. But here the democracy ended, the equality stopped. Gran's laatas ascended on long stately sticks they call "Ps" into the curved mouth of the heated brick oven. Mine descended to the zally at the back of the oven where the heat of the ashes gave them their slow browning.

Sunday morning Gran was stiff, regal and happy, hailing with loud good mornings every householder whose kitchen gave the fireside signal of being at home and awake. Long hurried steps, me running my short steps behind her, holding her hand, keeping pace with great effort; ribbon and streamers shaking, then flying with the too hurried movements. Then in church loud praying, lusty singing; nods and smiles, sunshine of goodwill; this more like a fair than a church service, man!

Mt Nebo was a Baptist church and I owe all my Sankeys to those long interludes at Gran. At home, in our Anglican softness, we mostly kept quiet, or gave brief responses to prayers and chants from the mouth of the priest. Baptist parsons were strong and black and fat to me then, their voices firm and protective and sweet. Our "fathers" at home were white and thin and weak with pale children playing in the churchyard in long socks. And sometimes the chants strained Father a little and he rendered strange, pitiable billy-goat tones. At Mt Nebo there was no chanting, just bible reading and honest, lusty singing. Now I think about it, that's the only church I have known where the regular service included a little speech from parson to the children and at least one hymn per Sunday specifically for children.

Of course the content was the same; and the intent was the same in both churches, no matter how each priest stage-managed his affairs. For where in the Anglican mode, as the men walked round with the collection plate, the priest would say: "Rend your heart and not your garment…" or "According as the Lord has prospered thee…", the Baptist hymn for the collection would include lines like:

> We work by our prayers
> By the pennies we bring
> By small self-denials
> The least little thing
> Can work for the Lord
> In His Harvest…

But in my scheme of things, the Baptist mode definitely had the edge. Listen to this now. I am not too sure at what point of the service this most important ritual took place. Perhaps while the adults were drinking wine from individual cups (an amazing sight to me bred in a one-holy-chalice system), I was allowed to walk towards the font and join some other children who were stretching their hands for things to eat from a white-clothed tray supervised by Goddy, an old lady who was a friend of my grandmother, the godmother of my mother and perhaps of every other young woman of her age for miles around.

There were totos and fine gizadas, coconut drops and Bustamante-back-bone (alias stagger-back) and I believe the finances were prearranged with mothers and grandmothers of the children around because I can't remember any money passing. Money in the house of the Lord is only allowed, in any case, to pass to the Lord. All in all, there was a lot more obvious joy in the piety in my grandmother's church than I ever found in ours.

And after church, endless talking in the churchyard, everybody wanting to know which grandchild this "fuu pickny"? and a nice round-face man laughing and saying: "Miss Eva a wudda wear jacket fih dis wan." You see at home there was the handshaking and everything, but the smiles for Father were purse-lipped embarrassed smiles while he shook your hand. And after all you were nothing special there, certainly no visiting grandchild and what is more you were hungry. Anglicans downright believed in starvation; even just think about the rule that says you musn't eat breakfast if you are going to take communion. At Baptist you could smile all day for all the children were laughing and your belly was full.

Besides, Gran was so important-looking that you felt good to be there and to be hanging around her. The bulk of her garments gave a kind of style, a kind of grandeur to Gran's step. One heavy tread with the black laced-up boots would cause the four layers of clothes to swing from one side to the next, touching the left then the right leg at mid-calf in a kind of rhythmic swing. (When you looked at Gran's laundry you thought she was washing clothes for a female contingent in some obscure army.) Her Sunday clothes: a white broadcloth skirt and either of several fancy white blouses with frills and tucks and all supported of course by her famous foundations. The house of the Lord deserved nothing but the best. You hardly noticed then the gnarled hands and bursting veins that ages of baking and ages of doing man's labour on the farm marked her with.

You noticed the elegant sombre ensemble, the eloquent eyes and mobile face, and perhaps, most outstanding of all, the straight back and squared shoulders. There was beauty and strength and very obvious pride in her carriage. When you own what you live on as far as eye can see, you owe no man, you trust and fear your God, you exude a kind of confidence that country people call pride, and that town people only hear about.

Gran was close to us with a closeness that parents can't really feel. A whole generation has to pass before blood links take on this passion. Parents with their concerns that are practical, that allow us to be all the things that make grandparents proud, can't afford it. Our school successes were Gran's personal victories. She expected them. Didn't her father leave her a blessing better than anything money could buy? Just as Isaac before his death blessed his Essau (or so he thought), so Isaac, her father, had blessed her:

"Your blessings shall flow like a river

Not unto your children, but to your children's children…"

She had neglected her seven when his death was approaching and with her young strength had nourished his weakness. She had brewed his favourite broths, read his favourite words from the Bible, sung him Sankeys and kept him company to the end… she the eldest, most loving most faithful. And to his blessing we owed all our successes; and every time we went to tell her we had passed something, or every time she read our names in the papers, she would hold her hands up to God and thank him for honouring her father's promissory note.

By the time I had read the Bible myself enough times I found that Isaac of old ended up with goat soup not venison and blessed his younger son dressed up as his elder son so it was quite all right that Gran, who supplied beef soup to her father and who was a daughter dressed in a man's job, minding her children single-handed, should receive the blessing usually reserved for the elder son. Though of course in this case there was no conniving wife or mother.

Where is my share?
Up in the air!

In the district there was a kind of awesome regard for Gran. She had a reputation for Christian morality that was more like a special telephone arrangement with God than like anything else. Her conversations with Him were impromptu, informal and evidently received immediate response. She could browbeat people, on the strength of this, into action they didn't even contemplate. I can still see Miss Mamma, short, thin and with a resigned smile on her face, climbing the hill with a basket on her cotta and Mass Nate bringing up the rear with his slow, bare-footed one two one two, a bunch of bananas on his shoulder and a cloth cap on his head. And the two little girls behind them now and then, beside them now and then, racing now and then to see who would reach Miss Eva yard first. They could have the two rooms, yes; Miss Eva had decided to rent them, but they had to stop living in sin. Hard-working, faithful, concubinal bliss was not enough for my grandmother. They took the rooms.

I remember the plain gold band on the cotton wool in the little white box. Gran showed it to me. She had dressed herself in all her finery and gone up to Tavern Hill to Mr. Matthew the jeweller and had taken the ring on credit. Of course, she made the down-payment, and these two people, who had never quarrelled with their state, were forced to conform and to dress themselves one righteous Wednesday morning for a quiet little thing at Parson's mission. And Sunday, poor Mass Nate, squirming in shoes and a suit he must have had since he was seventeen, took Miss Mamma to "turn thanks" in front of everybody.

So maybe you understand now how come Gran had to go and

ask the young green Parson Jones, younger than any of her sons, to strike her name off the church register years later when her own daughter moved into a state of faithful concubinage. You understand too why she started sitting at the back of the church and refused to take communion. Now of course you may say her daughter was forty and a free agent, you may even say that's no new big thing especially in this country, but that is because you don't know better:

"Gran –" I had said to her.

"Yes my daughter –"

"Your daughter's daughter –"

"Yes my daughter's daughter –"

"Wasn't Israel divided equally between the tribes that were descended from Jacob's children by his wives Leah and Rachel and the tribe descended from the children of his concubines who were the handmaids of these women?"

"Yes –"

"So what's the difference between concubines in the Bible and concubines now that you have to get so vex about this?"

"Young lady, don't you realise that that was the result of God's orders, the Almighty's orders?"

"Then how you know that this is not part of the Almighty's plan?"

Silence… silence…

"It isn't; you just believe me that it isn't –"

"But Gran, anybody hear you would think Aunt Pin invent this kind of living; you understand how many people would stop take communion if they was like you? Parson would get drunk every Sunday having to drink off the wine, him one."

"Every man to his own order. I am not them."

Clearly God had omitted to tell my grandmother that the rules were changing. His telephone connection with her had been silent on that matter.

Some people used to say she was too much like a man and like take things in her own hands. You see they didn't know she had been given special instructions through her telephone to heaven. When they said she was masculine, they couldn't mean her face though, for that was soft and mobile with a charm that was inescapably feminine. But the figure she cut if you got into an argument with her, or what she looked like from behind if you happened to catch her pose cutting a bunch of bananas, or showing a young man how to handle a sharp cutlass with power against the unfortunate cane, or merely hurrying through deep grass on a damp morning, each foot shrouded in heavy coarse boots, connecting with the ground with a frightening thud and half sinking in the stiff yellow clay... perhaps they had a point then.

I am not quite sure what a matriarch is; some kind of founder of a line, some large female inspirer marking off a crossroads on some time-map in a family or tribe. But for me, even with such an imprecise definition, Gran was a matriarch. I don't know whether it had to do with how she saw herself or with how others saw her or with some kind of interaction of the one with the other. In our house, for instance, whenever she visited, I think she saw herself as a kind of final word... *rex et legifer*, self-chosen arbitrator in family disputes. Witness her, while we at the junior table giggled, telling my father, closer fifty than forty: "You keep quiet, you just come out of eggshell!" as if comparative youth bestowed an obvious and shameful inferiority that only time could remove.

Gran wasn't a leaning and dependent kind of woman. It isn't easy to be leaning and dependent though when you have no one to lean on in that very special sense. For no matter how kind and well-meaning other people are, the relief of leaning can only come if the pole is the right one, and is the recognised support whose priorities are the same as yours; not my business first, then yours if I have time. And when a big strong man gives you seven children and quietly moves across to St. Peter's gate, you simply have to learn to "take care o' business" and that sometimes precludes the stance of coy fairlady... for who on a farm would listen to that and take it seriously? And I can't find anyone to tell me yet how you can be father and mother to a family of seven and still emerge the whimpering female. Besides, who says there is anything so grand about being able to whimper? My Ghanaian friend told me, years after the end of Gran and all that, that a matrilineal family structure allows woman the luxury of having a sense of self, not merely a sense of being her husband's rib. Perhaps it was a sense of self that Gran had that showed in her every look or step; and since the body of her rib had so long been gone anyway… at least they couldn't make it a curse on her.

We had heard tales from Gran's children, young aunts and uncles, of their unrelenting mother fighting constant battles with them against all the devil's pursuits: against dominoes and dancing and against all strong drink… "for he who is deceived thereby is not wise". She was in complete control and enforced her rules with a leather strap even after these young people had reached the long pants and the stockings stage!! Life was supposed to run within certain well-defined lines: school, church, work on the land or at the mill for a living. But can't a generous eye discern in the sternness a strong, simple determination to keep the ambition banner flying no matter what? How else could you afford the training to earn yourself a living if you didn't help earn the money? Who else was there to transport the bananas from bush to roadside so Mass Bredda cart could take them to siding? Who else to deliver the buns and the bullas to all the ginger-beer and sorrel restaurants between Benbow and Tavern Hill? I suppose I can talk because I didn't feel, but those sufferers, all they seem to remember is rush, rush, rush; help with the baking, rush! Deliver the bread, rush! Cut the canes, rush! Carry bananas in a one two hip-swinging movement down the hill; then wash you face, drink your tea, wrap up your chaklata and run, run, run, and look straight in teacher Green eye while you try to explain why you reach after roll-call again; that you mother is a man and that she pushing she one to make sure that you carve your name with pride one day and that neither you nor you brothers join the pile of old nyaga who can't make a living because they parents didn't make sure they come to something. And that you mother working on a promise she make to you father, her Corpie, who shut his eye and gone to St. Peter, but who sitting there like a dove on the top of that tomb to urge her to make everything go all right.

Corpie was a high rectangular tomb two chains or so from the oven-house and two chains or so from the pass that led up to the front door. But he was also everything else… How do you keep a man in your heart and in the general heart of your family years and years after his death? Ask Gran. For her eldest child had been nine when he died; in fact all that Lue remembered of him as a tangible memory was that he taught her to spell VEGETABLES and that since she could spell the TABLES part before, she thought that the whole word was VEGETABLE-TABLES and that the teacher didn't appreciate that word in her homework and made her know it in a very practical fashion. Lue always said that she felt cheated though, when he died, for they had a great father-daughter love thing going, which we all understand, whether we have been fathers or daughters.

Corpie had never really died, at least as far as Gran was concerned. He had been put in that tomb. But every time she had to make a big decision, she waited for him to put the solution in her mind or to send a sign. Sometimes I wondered how she knew when God and when Corpie was telephoning, but perhaps they were bound up, those two, her great lovers, in some kind of oneness; I don't know. I didn't ask her because that would automatically come under the heading of blasphemy and she was not encouraging the young generation in that. Corpie, in my mind-picture, had been a strapping, black six-footer with large, shiny shoes. And I was not a little put out by the squatness of his figure when Gran unearthed and hung on the wall a picture of his contingent in their khaki uniforms and unattractive braces. He had fought in the Boer wars. Gran had relayed to us his tales of beautiful African women with complicated coiffures that could last for weeks on end. And that was long before black women were allowed to be beautiful in our part of the world. I always wondered, though, how he felt, child of the empire, sent by his boss brother, to kill blood brother! Or isn't that what the war was about?

After that war he turned to farming and butchering and asked Gran's father for her hand, though he was several years older, a full man. He got consent and a blessing and the usual oration: "You have plucked a lily from my garden…"

"Lily?" I asked Gran, "Such a black lily?"

But she didn't take me on for I was flighty and foolish and supposed to be full of nonsense.

They rode together, she told me, from the house of her father, six miles uphill to the new land this man provided, he straddling the horse, she riding side-saddle, and reached it, Comfort Hall, one historical morning. The bright sun was forcing the mist from the valley. The hillsides were already green with the gold flame hovering over. She wore her hair in "puffs", she said, each braid plaited halfway, loose halfway. That coiffure had no aesthetic appeal for me but from all she said, he liked it; for him yes, so for her yes. And that's where they toiled and bore fruit and children for ten years; ten years and seven children, and then… Amen so let it be; the Lord God in heaven knows best; we mustn't fly in His face. But I felt it took all her faith not to fly in His face and all her control not to cry as she told me…

Corpie was there with Gran raising her children, seven and fatherless; seven for schoolbooks, seven for plates at meal-time, seven for illness. And in a real crisis he would appear in a vision.

Gran never tired of telling of the fateful dark night that was like ten nights together when Enid, no more than a toddler, lay writhing in pain, almost gasping for breath; of her slough of despair, without adult companion; no one to turn to; no doctor for twelve miles and even Dispenser, who cured almost anything, sleeping and snug in the dark rainy night. In any case how to reach him? How to desert all the others this dark lonely night? She dozed, she recalled, ever so briefly, and dreamt in that slight sleep she saw the dear Corpie who wordlessly led her where the large copper (retired from its role in the sugar-boiling business) sat waiting the roof-gutter's blessing. The rain had been light, persistent and light – white rain we call it – so the copper half empty; he showed her the water, its dull yellow surface sprinkled with manna – the seeds of the white coriander. She awoke, mixed coriander and water; her sick child was healed with two spoons of the substance. Call it magic, if you want, coincidence if you are cynical, but for Gran, God bless you Corpie, God's in His heaven.

Visions from Corpie always had water, in some shape or form. To Gran it all made sense when, years after his death, she kept her cool as she listened, facing with cloudless eye a penitent woman in tearful confession that she, in her anger, had caused Corpie's death, by poisoning one evening the bottle of water she knew he would drink in the heat of the next day... water sitting there clear in the corner, leaning against the bamboo in his hut. She had suffered. She was weeping. She had paid over and over for the sin she had committed. Sin triply cursed since the victim was innocent and totally ignorant of how he had offended. (A strange woman really. Usually people wait till their deathbed and confess through their pain right up to the last breath.) For Corpie had been a stranger in those parts and, trusting the truth of the documents, had bought land without knowing its history of quarrels; how many sisters and brothers and cousins all equally claimed it. She, frustrated, her rights overlooked, took the fates in her own hands and ended his ownership. And all in vain plus the weight on her conscience. She was sorry, she wept for the innocent widow and wept for the children seven and fatherless; but the fates had exacted their punishment from her, and after confessing, still sobbing and weeping, she was begging Miss Eva to give her an old frock to wear down to Linstead, so with some of the others she could take a last look at the face of her Captain. For she had turned to God, through the Salvation Army, and Captain, the chief of her army division, had suddenly died. A truckload of sisters was due for the funeral... "You want to see Captain face?" ... My grandmother's deep deep kindness didn't stretch to people like them.

That woman whom I never saw except through my grandmother's eyes haunted me, though. And every time I think about making a road through life and not looking to right nor left to see who you chopping down like high grass on the side of your road pass, I remember her. And I know that people weren't meant to live so. And sometimes I get blind and racial and blame whiteness and machines and say black people never born living so, and that no amount of bulldozer and milk powder should make them live so.

But I remember her, and remember that time was – long before bulldozer, long before milk powder – when some part of us had been hard, and grudgeful and naked evil; that if you search black people's experience you will find a lot of love, but you will also find a lot of dreadful deeds. For some people didn't get the message about love; perhaps they didn't get the message about retribution either...

How shall I reach it?
Climb on a broken chair!
Suppose I fall?
I do not care!!!

Some say that growing old is slow; that grey hairs creep upon us one then two, and then eventually too many for us to pay our grandchildren pennies to pull out. Others say it is quick – a thief at night, and imperceptible. Perhaps they are both right. Perhaps the body feels itself slipping away part by part; perhaps the effort to conceal the weakness and the novel frailty gets greater and greater week by week. But for those who look on it, it isn't a process at all; it is one day a sudden shock, a sudden realisation that sixty has gone and eighty has come.

So I remember me doubting Gran's sixty. A handsome old woman, an excited and doting grandchild – she depending on me for fulfilment, I depending on her for an ego inflation I didn't earn but was heir to – first child of her eldest child with her face written on me – each feeding the other in a re-enactment of the creation pattern again. She denying her youthfulness, refusing new teeth on the grounds of a grave too near to forget… "Teeth?" she had frowned, "Give me the money and I will plant you an acre of yam-head."

Then I remember an old lady dependent and leaning; now more hungry for my company than I for hers. I hadn't noticed the timing of the change of the need; time had been thief here, and subtle indeed. And the signs now clearer than ever, like arrows on a girl-guide trail; you only see them when you start looking and then you wonder how you didn't notice them before. A demand for the same teeth refused ten years earlier on the grounds of age; a sudden need for a black and white wig and frightening embarrassment at the loss of hair.

"If anybody ask you, Pet, 'Who is that?' say your grandfather, not your grandmother." The touching connivance to help us miss the bus and stay to quench the thirsty loneliness… the not-too-subtle ruses to demand our presence there; the walk no longer jaunty; fingers now not only gnarled but sometimes arthritic and useless… And for those who wished to see it, the irony of minding seven or seventeen, as if children were a safety device against old loneliness.

By the last rise of breathless hill I could hardly maintain the long stride, so I leaned on the tangerine tree to catch my breath. I didn't swing on the limb or rest there and call; all that belonged to another time. One final burst and I could hear my soles grazing the cobbles and silence. I looked in at the back door and couldn't tell in that split second whether relief or disappointment was what I felt. Seven miles of composing and recomposing myself for the first real adult test. Here I was, representing my mother in fact this time. The message had been urgent; my departure so hurried; transport unusual and haphazard: five miles in the front of a truck, one on the crossbar of a bicycle and the rest on my fast feet…

And all the time that nagging worry, the almost certainty with all its horror that Gran would die that night; there, next to me on her bed, with the deep and fearful darkness all around us… But there she was, sitting on a low wooden bench one foot immersed in a wooden tub half full of water, the other barely slipped in old broken-down slippers. She lifted her eyes from the page of the Bible while her hand still held the round magnifying glass over the letters, straining forward to make sure:

"My light has come," she said.

And I trying to hide all emotion: "How is it Gran?"

She had planned it she said… She knew she couldn't have my mother then, but knew by the calendar I was at home… After all the University holidays are that much longer than my mother's holidays…

So the rush, and the anxiety and the fear…

After that Gran's telegrams to our house were many. No longer were fond feet rushing downhill to meet an unexpected old lady climbing uphill with a tray full of bake-bake. Nobody now watched her quick fingers lessen the baskets of mending my busy mother always left for her, or sat around to earn the farthings she paid every time you had to thread the needle for her with your young eyes…

My father used to take the telegrams, after a while, and rest them on the organ in the drawing room till Mamma came from school; they were no longer urgent enough to disturb her work day, according to his judgement at least. A telegram was now no better than a letter marked URGENT – ignored by him as the mail man ignores such a signal. But my father used to joke that he hoped at least one of his sons would have an outside child and bring it home for them to mind. Or sometimes he would say they would adopt an Indian child… a little girl. (Perhaps since Indians were so scarce in our area, the whole thing was improbable enough for my mother to allow him his dream.) Clearly though, while we were loud and many crowding round him, he saw the fearful Bogey in the distance: the inevitable desertion and old age with loneliness.

And when my mother died, he made it clear that he felt he had lost more losing a wife than we ever could losing a mother… "You can't understand," he said, "how much I will miss… especially the talk…" and we did indeed remember them talking through the night and going over all sorts of old sharings…

Perhaps Gran had seen the Bogey too. Perhaps that is why she had tried with Abijah. Abijah was a legend from before my time. A legend without a handle on his name. I knew his old gramophone. That was still there within my memory times. You sort of turned a handle – like cranking an old time Ford – then you stuck the needle on and the thing gave the same sound you get if you squeeze your nostrils with your fingers and then try to sing. I had actually seen Abijah… One day when they sent us to collect Gran's coarse boots at Josephus the shoemaker and somebody had the bright idea to take me to show me Abijah. There he was, standing at his door that faced the road; a sallow faced old man with a slight paunch giving a rigidity to his braces… There he was, right there where he belonged, back in his own house half a mile from Gran's. He had gone back there after Gran discharged him and started forcing people to change back from her new married name to her old married name and getting offended if they didn't – though I feel sure she didn't ask the courts to do a thing about it… a completely informal arrangement. My father always said it was Gran's children who drove away Abijah and then they didn't want to deal with the vacuum he left.

And my own view of Abijah was completely biased. It had nothing at all to do with my personal judgement, for I did not know the man. But I accepted completely the view I got from the remnants of the Abijah jokes my mother's younger brothers kept alive. He was a green-verb man, and of course that couldn't be tolerated in a house where young men were offered books to read if they came to court the daughters of the house, who were busy studying for exams:

"I have givd this shop a kitchen!" was one of the favourite quotes. And Abijah was a lazy man…

"Miss V wants her tea and I wants mines too…" (Miss V being a baby staying at the house that time.) How could he survive in a book-struck household on a work-struck farm? While he read the Bible and witnessed for Jehovah, everybody else was cutting bananas or boiling sugar, or baking… or of course studying for some exam or other.

But perhaps Gran could have dealt with that. It was the Bible that attracted them and that hadn't changed. But when eyes look on critically, even the best alliances weaken… far more a weak one . . . So Abijah took his Bible and left and left his gramophone for me to laugh about.

And Gran became a neglected child playing out all the attention-getting tactics in the book and some not yet in the book. Seven children and umpteen grandchildren all playing out their own lives single-mindedly; after all her effort, after all her sacrifice. But the sacrifice had been love and duty; she wasn't giving tit to ensure tat. Thank God. Her sons write and send money, as if money is what matters… She wants more words. She can't accept the excuses that hide the admission that there is nothing to say. Last letter at Christmas or Easter traced as many life trends as they are willing to share now. The rest for their privacy earned at long last.

Her daughters write but visit only rarely. Everyone lives far away and everyone is busy. A trip home takes planning and the leave and the money to bring the family too so she can see the grandchildren. Except Lue; well she lives quite near and has two big daughters. So she can get the urgent letters and telegrams for it isn't so difficult for somebody to rush up and provide company for at least a night, until they get her to the doctor if they insist, until he says it's no grave illness only pressure again and gives her more pills. And they make the usual offer to take her home with them. Isn't it a little like crying wolf? Isn't she afraid they won't react after a time? No. They will come. Perhaps not right away but they will… for suppose this was the last call… what a life-sore on their conscience!

No, she can't live with them. It isn't the same you know, being cock of your own roost and being cockerel in somebody else's. All attempts have been short-lived and each one worse than the last at that. The lifestyles are different. Lots and lots of little habits okay in your own house just don't make it in somebody else's too strict, too lax, too sad, too gay…

And old age is eccentric just as youth is intolerant…

Well somebody should live with her then… Who?… So everyone looks at the least prosperous of the children; the only self-employed one and all rationalise that she could manage as well in the country as she does in town. Why me, she asks. And everyone pretends to forget that she in her youth ran away to the city to the bright lights… to escape the dull sameness of the district she knew…

When my mother died, it seemed that everyone was trying to prove that everyone else was more responsible for her working so hard and dying so early. Not Gran. I remember her terrible quietness through the whole day. Then I remember her falling completely apart at the funeral, not crying or anything, just hanging about the coffin and asking that they open it one more time so she could put a flower on Lucy's breast before they moved from the Community Hall to the Church. And I remember me, losing patience with her, being short with her for obstructing the men in their business. I didn't want any delay. I was embarrassed to watch her act out her unshed tears while I fumbled with my grief and frustration. I was angry at her for letting the side down, for doing what I so badly wanted to do. I should instead have praised her control, control that prevented the wild thrashing about that older people sometimes allow themselves at funerals. And I of all people should have understood. For I had been so near to her all the years…

"What will happen to me now?" she had whispered in anguish… "I should have died before her." And a look of despair, of wild frustration gathered in vague wateriness about her eyes…

She moved in with us. It was clear that there was a crisis and some woman was needed in the house. And she was the obvious volunteer. She would stay and fill Lue's place. And she couldn't see her age and her frailty, so she couldn't sense the irony we saw in the matter.

She had moved in with us before, on earlier occasions. But it never worked over protracted periods. The time gap and the orientation gap had made it difficult. We were the devil's children sometimes, with too much self-possession. My brothers were free to eat things when they liked without asking. Gran never understood that the home of a working mother evolves its own rules that look like licence to other eyes. We played the devil's music on God's day… and if she fell asleep with her mouth slightly open, the young ones would put grass straws in. And they resented all attempts at control:

"Vel, you think that old lady hate me?"… She must have heard; they didn't understand…

This time was different and far worse. Her habits were now very old and single. When you live alone you can mix a long drink and taste with the mixing spoon if you like, for you are always the drinker now and tomorrow. The wandering brain of old age doesn't allow you to change to accommodate community living. So you taste with your spoon and the children, suddenly silent, don't drink. See how stupid it all is though. You kiss a man you hardly know and you swear he is germ-free, but you are sure you can't drink what your Granny's spoon taste…

But worse, her attempts to replace Mamma in planning and

running the house! She couldn't do it and you couldn't correct her… so our nerves and Papa's nerves couldn't stand it…

She got the message, somehow, and returned to her lonely, solitary nest, to her large and now comfortless hall, now that Corpie and Naomi and Lue were dead and she could see no sense in it at all…

Time is one distance, space is another, and how you see things yet another. Every new year of our lives, every new stage of our lives and our experience, lengthened and stretched out each of these distances between Gran and ourselves. We took all this for granted, as we took so much else for granted. She felt it. Add to this her own mind distancing itself from itself… You didn't have to be there to hear her hissing her teeth in annoyance at her own acts of petty forgetfulness… You could feel it equally in the disconnected phrases her letters became… I remember her last letter to me. Couldn't have been long before her mind sealed itself away. I was miles in distance. But she wrote, and enclosed, as if in token of a last clarity, the last fruits, she said, of my favourite aniseed tree behind the house… "the last of the crop" I read; and a great fear filled me that another last was near… But that worry was not to be yet…

My final guilt-ridden visit to that great old lady dogged me through young womanhood to maturity, years after she had taken up residence in heaven running errands for her God. My mother was perhaps four years buried, and I was visiting – a fleeting visit – all I could manage from my exile then. Comfort Hall a mere dot on my busy schedule.

Gran was beautiful, as always, her face smooth and unlined, a cloth hiding her short grey hair except at the edges. She wore a pleated shirtwaister, American cut, sent by my aunt no doubt. She was lying on her side, alone in her room… I stared and stared and kept marvelling at her skin, still glowing, no ashen overlay as you learn to expect on the very old… She babbled something incomprehensible, not the slightest gleam of recognition in her vague eyes… An old male cousin was in charge; the only other person there that evening. She had been kind to him, as she had been to many others, in her own stern fashion. Besides, he needed the house to live in and the land to farm. But he didn't like looking after her... and he complained that she was old and miserable, yes far older than he, and that her children should take her to live with them... though he knew that whole, long story...

I wanted to stay, and felt I should stay at least the night and put things in order the way she liked me to in the old days when I loved the calmness of the holidays there: tidy her drawing room, put new flowers in the vases, change her pieces of old crochet work for other pieces of old crochet work smelling of Khus Khus root from her special chest in the corner... and straighten the chairs, dry-rotting now from lack of use... I knew I should stay at least until a glimmer flashed in her mind and she recognised me... But I couldn't, for my sins. I had to hurry to catch the bus back to my own life, my own children waiting in the city this brief holiday. I, like her children before me, was pursuing single-mindedly my own life, my own family...

Children and grandchildren are lent to us to do for them in their need, but the frightening isolation of the human being and the cruel distances we can't help making are the truths that belie such sacrosanct platitudes as "age is honour". For honour is very cold...

And when I knew all that, I wanted to indulge my own children with myself while their need was there; for their need would be short-lived with no clockwork to decide how short... and then the need would diminish just as mine for her had, and the pain would be so much less, if each moment had been fulfilled...

> Children children
> Yes Mummah
> Where have you been to?
> Grandmummah
> What did she give you?
> Bread and Pear...

My bustling grandmother and my lonely grandmother had both gone. There was now not even the little ruse now and then to find company. There was no company to find anyway... All the little chickens who had risen up betimes had gone forth... had become fowls and had hatched their own chickens, but foreign chickens, industrial chickens who couldn't sit on a hot stone and wrap their skirts around their knees, couldn't sing Sankeys and drink mint tea from tin cups, who had no individual names but were just "the children"! And if you offered them your sweet Larena cane from the house-side, you bet they would ask for a knife!

Now the plotting was mostly on the other side. How to get Gran away from home if her mind was working? How to persuade her to stay in the city? And when she did stay, how not to grow conscience-stricken at the restless, near terrified look on her face because she longed for hills that were grass not asphalt and for water that was tangy with the taste of the roof. They tell me she was restless, too, with worry, whenever they kept her in town, lest she draw her last breath anywhere but on the land that had known the joy and the sorrow that had made her in fifty years or more. So her dreams were harsh and terrified nightmares there in the city, where the best doctors were found... unless of course you know that doctors and medicine are, most of the time, in the mind...

The face on her in the city was agonised; not the smooth face and brow I had seen, the face that wrinkled only when the vague eyes searched my face for a sign to help them pick me out in the confused file of images three generations deep... Her home face was at peace and would be so till she made the almost imperceptible transition from this life to that...

I was doing my penance out in the land of whiteness and success – where they were asking me for the black opinion – when the news of Gran's death came to me. But I heard it as if a voice from a hollow tree spoke nonsense words to me. For I knew there was no truth in it. My grandmother had died years before; quietly, without telling anybody, she had taken her spirit, while she still possessed it, up into the clouds to her God and let them take the body where they would. I knew that from the time I heard that she had been taken to live in a place her spirit couldn't possibly inhabit, her daughter's house in the city, filled with strange and Godless people, a house full of music of old John the devil, her arch-enemy, a house where there were children born without the benefit of the church... And other spirits had taken over her vacant body, and the discord of the union made sounds. So when they wrote to say the pressure gone up in the old lady head, I knew what they were misinterpreting... So they took her to hospital and there the unresisting body ceased to be...

At the funeral, I hear, her sons sang loud and deep laments swinging the coffin back up the hill with their great strength; bringing her back with solemn noises to a place she had never left... for she had outsmarted them at the last and with the help of God had gone up to him closing her eyes on green grass, the cane patch and Corpie's tomb, and with angel voices singing softly in her ears...

> Little children little children
> Who love their redeemer
> All the bright ones
> All the gay ones
> His loved ones his own...
>
> ★
>
> They shall shine in their beauty
> Bright gems for his crown...

The fog had risen completely from the valley and the new sun had turned the fallow field inch by inch into a lush, light-green carpet. Beyond that, on the right, the land descended into a circle which marked the end of one, the beginning of another holding. On the left, the metal trunk of the cane-mill, like a work of art from an early civilisation, sat silent with its wooden arms ill-fitting and unsuitable, far too long for such a stubby trunk, dangling in the dust of the very last season's dead and juiceless cane.

If you were quiet, as I was, and let the morning sounds come to you, the last of the birds would pick up the echo of the years and quickly yoke a cow or a horse to those long and useless wooden limbs, would show the bulging muscles of the smooth-skinned black strong man in his flour-bag vest, feeding the cane between the black and heavy metal gums, confident that barrel on barrel of yellow liquid frothing white would pour from the bamboo gutter set there to receive it. You would hear the occasional crack of the whip as the same patient man suddenly felt an urgency from some unpredictable source and forced the animal to trot more quickly, and force the gums to press more firmly and the liquor to flow more freely, cascading in tiny torrents over each hump of the bamboo joint and threatening to spill but never quite keeping the threat.

Or you could look at the silent, broken-down top of a forgotten thatched hut and see rockets of smoke shoot upward from a white-marl chimney while the smell of boiling sugar sweetened miles and miles of air. You can't go too near the huge copper bubbling with the thick rich brown liquid sugar, for everyone knows there is one kind of burn you don't ever survive – the boiling-house burn. So you wait till the large, well-dressed, barefooted, right-hand man with the little crocus handbag over his shoulder, stretches up tall and unhooks long, half-tunnels of bamboo filled with sweet sticky butterscotch candy that you can't quite connect with everything else there. Wait till he smiles his large shy half-smile and curls what looks like miles of the stuff on your private bamboo spoon.

I always wondered about this sugar-boiling right-hand man. I never saw any money pass from Gran to him, though there is no rule that says that even my inquisitive eyes see everything. But every morning, whether there was sugar boiling or not, he passed through the yard in clothes unusually clean for a labouring man, stained perhaps, but clean, with his little crocus shoulder-bag carefully slung and a clean short cutlass peeping out through the top right, under his arm. And his ten toes on the ground as if to deny the rhythm of his clothes:

"How is the morning, Miss Eve?"

"Fine thanks, Brother Jack… and how you?"

"Thank God, Miss Eve –"

"And Miss Clemmie, how she feeling this morning?"

"Not bad thanks, Miss Eve –"

I never saw Miss Clemmie. But I have a picture of a woman, half an invalid, shuffling about enough to wash and cook and mend but not enough to ever leave her house – the other half of a relationship that left just enough space for what he shared with Gran, too flimsy to harm a soul… If there is anything like a platonic relationship, a caring relationship between two old people who never thought of Eros, Gran and Brother Jack had it.

I'm sure he never knew Corpie, but I'm equally sure he sort of felt that Corpie had given him a sacred mandate to look after Miss Eva in a kind of way and supply a kind of man presence around the house... especially after the Abijah fiasco.

And when bun-making time came, his bun was always special; and if she had a morning-work, he would be there helping with the action and cheering on the other men. There are all sorts of farm jobs that even a strong woman can't do. She can't raise a new boiling-house; she can't patch the new mortar on an oven; she can't move a latrine... Sometimes she needs a man.

A little ridge overlooks the circle that is the boiling-house circle. It is a ridge so near to it that surely it must have been designed as part of it, or built itself by chance when the dirt piled up as they dug for the boiling-house. Soft grass grows there and little children sit and lick their bamboo spoons or early women sit there and talk the day's weariness away. And children who are inquisitive sit near them and hear whole heaps about life they won't be able to piece together till a long time after...

Nobody knows how the women know exactly when the huge boiler stops bubbling and brother right-hand man starts distributing new sugar. But they know. Perhaps the smell of sugar boiling near its end is very different from the smell of cane liquor boiling early or of light syrup forming halfway through. And they come. The women, empty handed; their pans have been there from the day before. When you order a can of sugar, you ask what day the skip will draw.

So now the pans are standing there in different lines according to rank or size. First row, zinc pans which various dealers will come today or tomorrow to take away on donkeys for the market; second row, butter pans each with its little initial or secret mark so Miss Angie won't take Miss Beatrice pan. Then the Ovaltine tins, as if that is the sort of maximum a single man can drink in tea and "bebridge" for a week or so. Last but not least, the gift pans including yours, you visiting grandchild, yours and those of a host of Gran's little godchildren in the district, the row of personalised condensed tins... A bout of sugar, always to me like Christmas...

so much work, so much excitement and the whole thing finished in a breath almost. By the time the pans cool, the sun has long gone down and the women have lit their bottle lamps to light the impossible paths to their homes. The cow, moving like a moon-struck zombie in the cane-trash circle, has become this morning's business; the sweet smell has become fainter and fainter and will eventually disappear... and all that is left of the reaping of the cane and all that subsequent activity is the row of stark tins with the liquid hardening in them... unless you stretched your mind and thought about each private thrill as the beverage, which only wet sugar can make, caresses each throat and drives away the midday thirst of tomorrow...

The mill-yard had bustled with people, had bustled with business once, but that too had sunk, like Gran, into a deep and endless coma. The metal trunk now looked like something struck in bronze...

The difference between the word and its representation on the page is not always appreciated by the reader, largely because by the time we come to think about things like this we are already literate in at least one language and have learned to match word with representation in a one-word-one-sound relationship. We say the representation is standardised because over the years a particular word-shape has come to be associated with a certain sound, conveying a certain meaning.

The business of writing the creole languages spoken by the bulk of people in the Caribbean islands is new. Early writers used English or French or Dutch or Spanish exclusively. After all, those were the official languages of the islands even though most of the people did not speak them. And most of the people still don't. What the people have always spoken are creoles which are lexically related to those European languages. Linguists have provided detailed analyses which show how different the creoles are from the European parent languages in sound and word order.

The popular language in Jamaica is Jamaican Creole (JC), an English related creole, the result of the interaction of English and several West African languages in a plantation situation.

Inevitably, as writers of fiction sought greater accuracy in their representation of character, the need to use Jamaican Creole became clear, just as the need to use other native languages even to a limited degree was becoming clear to writers in other linguistically complex situations.

The problem of presenting on the page a language which is without a tradition of writing, and so one which is not standardised, has existed ever since West Indians began to try to represent authentic Caribbean voices. Linguists have the easy recourse to using a phonemic script but the average reader would have neither the training nor the patience to read this. And so without any agreement as to how sounds should be represented, writers have tried to set down something which is recognisable to people who read English but which reproduces the sounds of the creole.

So for example the equivalent of the English word "there" might be represented as "dere", "deh", "de" or even there. The language itself, because it allows several sounds to convey one meaning and one sound to convey several meanings, is troublesome for the foreign reader. In addition, the fact that language tends to vary with situation and with social class lends further complexity to the matter. However, the answer cannot be to translate everything into English, especially as there are people in Caribbean society who do speak English and who need to be represented in that way.

Representing speech, especially in a situation where creole and standard language are lexically related, is difficult. If my own attempts to come to terms with it have proved confusing, I apologise.

Where in this collection I have used forms of speech which are different from English, I have simply written as I speak when I use JC. Sometimes, for example I write "a" and sometimes "I" to express the equivalent of the English "I". That is the way I speak. I know for example that you can't be emphatic with "a" in the way you can be with "I".

The creoles have flourished in the oral tradition and the attempt to write them is comparatively new. In fact when West Indians started to write stories, they wrote in English and depended on readers to select the intonation as they read, from their knowledge of the character. We have come a long way since then.

Some of you will still be alive when a standardised writing system for Jamaican Creole will have emerged.

Velma Pollard April 1989

NOTES

beeny – tiny (cf. Beeny Bird)

chaklata – solid food eaten a few hours after the early morning hot drink

cotta – a circular pad (about six inches in diameter) traditionally made of plantain or banana leaf or twisted cloth, worn on the head to steady a heavy load

laata – a sheet of tin; used as a large baking pan

prekkeh – somebody one easily takes advantage of

siding – small station where train stops specifically for loading bananas

zally – opening at back of oven into which hot ashes escape

CONSIDERING WOMAN II

For women everywhere
and in memory of Osmond Watson, artist and friend
who appreciated women and believed in my craft.

BITTER TALES

RUTHLESS AT NOON

If you were walking along the main road you would hear it. But you wouldn't be able to see who was singing

> We plough the fields and scatter
> The good seed on the land
> But it is fed and watered
> By God's almighty hand
>
> All good things around us
> are sent...

And you would hear the deep melodious bass stop and you wouldn't know why.

But if you were hiding your slight eight-year-old body behind the cabbage palm tree and looking down beyond the trench to the neat yam hills so recently weeded you would see a young woman, barefooted, wearing a faded shirtwaister dress, stretch her hand out to offer a package – a clean calico cloth tied over two enamel plates one on top of the other – through a break in the fence to the singer, Deacon, choir master, foundation of the church, upstanding citizen. You would see him take the proffered package with his left hand and with the other stronger right, pull the young woman over. You would notice him pay scant attention to the package after he has rested it on the pile of grass he had so recently weeded from among the yam hills.

You would see Deacon take a quick look around and apparently see nobody. Indeed why would he see anybody, least of all you, on top of the hill behind the cabbage palm trunk. He quickly unbuttons his fly with one hand. (Is he about to urinate in front of her?) You watch the young woman turn as if to run but the strong right hand pulls her and shoves her on to the ground, the bare ground, and begins to struggle with her underwear. She is kicking and his left hand is over her mouth. You feel a scream begin in your throat, then you think better of it. From where you are you can see that the hem of her dress is soon almost up to her neck. Then you don't see her any more only Deacon going up and down as if he is pumping the church organ with his whole body. Is he never going to stop, you wonder.

Beyond them is a pile of cassava sticks waiting to be planted. You could imagine leaves barely sprouting from some of the joints. Slight green on the brown, almost maroon.

Eventually Deacon does stop, gets up and strips pieces from a dry banana leaf, wipes the legs of the young woman who is standing now and not trying to run away any more but keeps her head down. She is gazing at the cassava pile. She pulls some more banana leaves and wipes herself again, roughly. She is sure to scrape her skin. He wipes himself, buttons his pants and sits down to undo the cloth wrapping the plates and to put the top plate on the ground beside him.

The young woman leaves him and walks along the pass. You recognize Missis, the maid in Deacon's house.

Deacon drinks water from a long bamboo joint and starts to work again. And to sing:

All good things around us
Are sent from heaven above
Then thank the Lord, oh thank the Lord
For aaaaahl his love

One rainy Friday when few children are in school and the teachers are having a meeting and middle division is allowed to do what it wants, Biddy (who they used to call, ambiguously you thought years later, Big Puss), the biggest and oldest girl in the class, who protected you from aggressors in exchange for your doing her sums under the desk when teacher wasn't looking, produces pencil and a dirty piece of paper and says she wants to draw something to show you. You don't know, she says, and you better get to know, how people get children. The disconnected lines soon become a man on top of a woman. You only recognize the woman because of her hair. But you are sure of the man because she draws his you-know-what on the outside of his pants almost as if it is falling off the picture. Then she writes in a terrible scrawl "Soon put it in" and shows you and giggles.

The next cut. On another piece of paper the woman alone. Same woman. Same hair style. But with a very big belly. Scrawl again "Six monts afta".

Final cut the woman with a baby. One breast is hanging loose and the baby is sucking it. "Nine monts afta".

For a split second you contemplate correcting the spelling but think better of it. You spend most of the time looking at the first cut and ask her if you can keep it. NOO she insists and smiles in a conspiratorial fashion. Her tongue squeezes itself through the space where she is missing a tooth. You always find it funny when she does that.

"You might go get me in trouble."

Your mind goes to Deacon but you don't say a thing.

Myra is deacon's daughter and she is your friend. Sometimes. Something had told you that you shouldn't let her know what you saw although you used to share most of your secrets with her.

One day Myra tells you that Missis not working with her family any more. Say her mother cuss her off and throw her things out of the room. You ask why. Myra say nobody tell her anything but her mother call all kind of words like "slack" and "lie" and "slut" and Myra gone with her belly swell up big big.

The last thing she do was chop up a set of cassava stick that was in the kitchen. They was waiting for Deacon to plant.

Years after you thought about it and wondered how many lunch times, after that time that you saw, did Deacon do it to Missis? What could she have done if she didn't like it? Could she have told the wife of the Deacon of the church that she couldn't take the holy man's lunch to the field because she was afraid of what he would do? Could she have simply refused to go and lose her job because she was disobedient? What if she had grown later to like what he did and didn't mind going. Does it really matter which was the case?

She must have told her employer eventually when there could be no further hiding the belly. So she became either a slut, for having tempted him, or a liar for having suggested he would do such a thing or both, in some convoluted sort of way.

And how would Missis feel towards the child she would bring? The child who caused her to lose her job; the child who, ironically, would be dependent on her for the very things only a job can buy?

But at the time all you did was wonder what would happen to Missis and why she chop up the cassava stick.

"ORINTHIA IS THAT YOU?"

It was first of August Fair. That time Emancipation Day was big. That time we were still one people glad for freedom not yet out of many one. And everybody was there. Certainly anybody who was anybody.

Fair day sounds were all around. "Frisco Frisco buy you frisco!" a man was shouting, agitating the metal rod through the cover of his pan to make a wicked local milk-shake. Children and adults were crowding around him. "Mango ripe it bound to drop," the one with the hawk's bill nose was saying as he bent over his table shaking the dice in a leather case and then throwing them out, inviting gamblers to try their luck.

The man with the ice cream bucket and cones didn't say a word but every next step he had to stop to scoop out ice cream with the shiny spoon and arrange it deftly on the cone in response to "single" or "double" from child or adult.

Jonathan George Jewbarry remembered his last cone ever. He was thirteen years old sitting on a country bus on a journey to Linstead to visit his grandmother. He had been licking the ice cream off, savouring it and looking out the bus window at the milling Saturday evening aftermarket crowd. Having finished the ice cream he was eating the cone. His teeth hit on something different. It was a rusty bottle stopper stuck in the funnel. Even now he grimaced at the memory.

His focus turned to the present. It was a yellow day, bright yellow against a pale blue sky without a single cloud. It was a picture-postcard day. But wasn't that how everyday seemed to him since his return?

Heads turned to watch the tall dark stranger step down from his buggy. A man in his prime. Elegant cutaway suit, gold chain leading into his pocket watch, J.G. Dewberry walked towards the food booth. The appearance of what people call pomp and ceremony was hardly diminished by the fact that he was himself the driver today and was going to buy his own food. He stood out in this gathering of ordinary people leaning their elbows on the huge slab of wood that was the makeshift counter, their heads almost touching the yellow and brown coconut leaves hanging from the thatched roof.

"One plate of curried goat, with bananas, no rice," he said in an accent only slightly tinged with Yank.

The woman behind the counter finished serving the current customer and turned her attention to him, the laughter from the last quip still on her lips. Suddenly the laughter died; her mouth fell open. Their eyes made four.

He collected himself first

"Is that you, Orinthia?"

There had been just enough time to close her mouth.

"Is that you, George Jewbarry?" she came back, quick as a flash.

He was remembering the softness of that skin. Not just what he could see now, her face and hands, but all over. Fifteen years fell away like a day and he still remembered the sensation. She could have been sixteen; a schoolgirl (euphemism for maid) in the Georges' house. He used to go upstairs there for lunch everyday.

He couldn't help himself. Twenty years old with his biology upon him. He had taken his plate to the kitchen himself that day. There was nobody else in the house. She was putting away plates on the shelves. She turned to fill her hands again. He put his arm across the corner.

"Mr. Barry?…" He put one finger of his free hand on his lips, then put the hand over the top of her dress. The breasts were ample and firm. He put his lips on hers quickly, fearing that she might clench her teeth. She tried to fight him off at first. Then she stopped struggling. Her body soon relaxed. He took her. Right there on the kitchen floor. He surprised even himself.

It was the first of many. Never again on the floor though.

Never again without her consent either. After that it became theirs, not just his. He became a man then. Physically. Learned to please a woman. Maybe she became a woman too. Learned to please a man.

When her clothes started to look tight he did not feel responsible. Certainly not in a way to affect his plans. He was going to America. To wash plates and get a profession. Yes he might have to wash plates. With luck he would get a scholarship eventually. The letters said that. He had been accepted at one of the best. Mr. Barry. She didn't seem to expect anything either. She certainly made no demands. She was definitely showing by the time he left.

A letter had come. She must have had to pay somebody to write it. "I name the child Aminata. We call her Taa."

He had never answered that letter.

A young girl was helping with the serving. Thick engine hair like her mother's, firm breasts and a flawless black complexion.

"Taa, this is Dr. George Jewbarry. Miss Essie nephew."

"Pleased to meet you, Sir." The girl lowered her eyes and shook his outstretched hand. He could feel the blood rush to the roots of his hair. This was no way to meet a daughter, he was thinking. He needed time.

He stretched his hand for the plate.

"Orinthia, we must meet and talk some time. So much to catch up on."

"I live at 20 Nugent Street. As Mrs. MacKenzie. Ask anybody where Mack the tailor live."

A smile played about her mouth as he walked away. Let him know she was Mistress MacKenzie. She belonged to somebody. She and her child were not outa door.

He could have ruined her. His future was not in danger. When she went home with the belly her mother was angry. She really had thought her daughter would have done better than she had done. She had got pregnant early. She thought her daughter would have been different. She had sent her to Miss Essie as a schoolgirl to learn to do things nicely: set table, cook certain foods they didn't eat.

"We wasn't looking for you there," she had said.

It was her grandmother, her mother's mother who said, "You fall. A no you first. Leave the baby with me. You buck you toe and fall down. Get up, brush off you frock tail and go on again." She had gone back out to work. This time with an even more hoity-toity family. Afternoon tea on the verandah. Napkins with hand embroidery. The cook taught her to make all kinds of fancy things.

Mackenzie was the carpenter fellow that did odd jobs for the house. She didn't hide it from him when he started courting. She told him she had a child. "Alright, what is yours is mine," he said. The rest was History as they say.

"So why Orinthia didn't kick Jewbarry in his groin?"

"Hormones eventually, though not at first. Or as the people say "her loins'. She was a young woman you know; and he was not uncomely. It wasn't any old white man as some of our forebears had."

"All the same, in the end it really didn't keep her back. The carpenter married her. And it seems by the time the good doctor found her she had a flourishing food business."

"Mmhm. Except we know what could have happened in between. She could have suffered when she left the job. Her mother could have put her out. Some of them did that."

"Yes. And he would never know."

GLEAN(H)ER ET CETERA

The smell of Sunday too-early morning. Before the Anglicans arise to go sing lustily in the old camp hut. She puts the *Gleaner* near the door; *Sunday Gleaner* prepaid. But the door opens and quick as a flash a strong hand on her unsuspecting arm. Someone is grabbing her. Too shocked to scream. Eventually she tries. But not a sound comes. In any case the towel stuffs itself in past her teeth. His own teeth grins, "You going to like it."

A slim girl looking no more than sixteen years old in a washed-out cotton frock, looking like a modern-day Mary McGuire (who stole two loaves of bread to feed her siblings and drove the judge to tears) walks slowly with her head down and a bundle of newspapers under one arm. Pass the Anglicans going to early morning church in their red gowns, pass the few Catholics returning from Mass. Clutching in the other hand a five-shilling note she is trying to think what that young man thinks she can do with that.

It hurt bad. This must be what her grandmother had warned her about. But is the same grandmother send her to deliver the already paid-for newspaper.

Grandmother sure to say is a lie, for those nice young men at UC who going to turn doctor could NEVER do such a thing.

"Madge, I never know you would so lie. Tell me the name of the little dry-eye gutter-rat that breed you. I sure him can't pay for the shirt on him back."

She had put the five shilling bill in an Ovaltine tin behind the safe. But it didn't have anybody's name on it. She didn't know the name of the man. She was not even sure if she saw him again she would know him. She hadn't delivered the paper again.

Granny really used to go herself. It was only that that Sunday she hadn't been feeling well.

He must have looked through a back window to note that she and not Granny would be at the door that time.

"Jesus lover of my soul… it hot."

"You didn't think it was hot when you were doing it?"

"Nurse, you don't know the half."

"Well tell me noh. And the whole. You little force-ripe girls are all the same."

"Oh Gawd…"

"Keep your breath. Stop screaming. Save the breath and push… Now!!!"

Wonder why women so hard on each other. Every story about midwives at lying-in is the same. And you would think that after all the talk about rape and child-abuse and senseless sex they would put two and two together and get some answers.

It is easier this way though. Blame somebody. The young girl. Then you don't have to think about it. Don't have to worry about society. In fact the man behind the abuse may be your own. Well not exactly that abuse, that female child, but some other one.

You think after those days it stop? And you think that is when it began? The difference now is that you can seem to care. Just wear the pin that says, "I make a difference."

Look at little Valdine. The little twelve-year-old from Spanish Town. Never know what hit her. As the press report it, both the uncle and the boarder in the house had been having their way with her for months if not years and when she try to tell her Aunt she see the uncle behind the Aunt moving his finger across his throat, meaning he would kill her if she ever talk so she just say, "Nothing Mam."

But what really kill me in that case is that the men out on bail waiting for the case to come up and she out there with nobody responsible, getting bigger and bigger and walking like she have hot orange between her legs.

After the newspaper call the public's attention to it, some place of safety take her.

Long ago I used to hear that men with venereal disease believed that if they slept with a virgin they would get cured (that is in addition, of course, to passing it on to her). Now I hear they also use them to test whether they are still fertile. A nurse told me about this eleven-year-old who had a miscarriage, crying in the hospital saying, "The man going vex, say im seed spoil."

Tell me about ignorance.

Found in high places sometimes you know.

I heard with my own ears (whose else?) a venerable judge (male of course) saying rape not so bad because is only a question of introducing the girl to something she will have to do later anyway. You hear me? I don't know if he has a daughter. And I don't know if he feels the same way about sodomy. That time all I said was, "Excuse me, let me go outside and be sick." But I was living then in a society that has its own rules (or lack of them) and they were already asking me (between guffaws) if I wanted to change things.

LORITA FROM COPPER

You see that woman walking and talking to herself like she mad? The one with the long skirt and dirty headtie. Well she mad. But don't look at her slight. Come off a good table you know. Every time I see her I feel to cry. You never know blood could so cruel to blood.

Both her mother and father used to teach at Copper. Father was the headmaster there. Then the mother get a chance to be a head-teacher too so she decide to leave Copper and be the head teacher at the school at Newlands. You don't know Newlands? Is near down to Linstead. So she leave, but the children, a boy and three girls stay at Copper since they was in school there and everything. The mother used to come up every weekend at first then it turn to every month end and then she stop come regular, just now and then. I don't know why.

Meanwhile the father, that's the head-teacher, start to visit a dressmaker lady who come to live in the district; visit just in a friendly way you know, since she was new. I remember my father, who had a lively interest in people business, saying that that wouldn't be him because dressmaker bed always have on too much pin. The lady have two sons. She come there with them. I don't even know if they were the same father. One much older than the other and both of them carry her name. So the headmaster start to sort of stand in for the father, especially since the older boy a little wayward. And the mother start to help out with organizing his life since the wife not coming up so often. She sort of stand in for the wife. At least that is how it look.

It mean that her sons was always at the cottage (so they used to call the headmaster house in those days). In fact the one that was about the age of teacher oldest daughter was taking lesson to turn teacher too. He did out school and was a sort of pupil teacher. That time after you out school at fifteen you could stay on and do exams they call Pupil Teacher Exams and either go to Teachers' College or just keep on teaching as untrained teacher.

As ah say teacher have three girls and a little boy. The oldest girl was still in school and she was very bright. She had already passed the exam the boy was studying for. They used to study together chiefly under the cellar. Cellar is what they call the space under those houses that build high off the ground. Don't confuse it with wine cellar for another climate and another class. In fact these older children bullied away the space from the little sisters and their friends who used to play dolly house under there, using the spring of the old sofa for bed, and the old chair and table for dining room.

To cut a long story short, it seems that during or after the studying – who to tell they – used the bed spring for serious purposes when no one was watching. In my mind the boy introduce her to it. And I say so not just because I am a woman, but I was in class with Lorita and she was fairly simple when it come to those things. She was very bright in her lessons, but she was always reading. She never come with us when we get away at recess time and go pick guava or break almond. So she wouldn't know the things we used to whisper about. The boy mother was hoping that she could help him bring up his marks. Well, him help her bring up something else.

I don't think she even fully understand what happen. I don't know what the fellow tell her before, for they always have some story. And as she was young and it was a first pregnancy nothing show for a long time. The uniform was a tunic with a kind of Empire Line so your body was a straight line down from under your breasts. And I don't think she tell anybody because she didn't have any close friend at school. You know how those bright children use to stay.

Nobody seem to notice anything or if they notice they wasn't saying, neither her father nor the dressmaker lady. One weekend her mother come up and there are many different versions of how she find out. Some say the two of them were in the kitchen outside and people who live near hear the sound from there. The mother let out one scream it would curdle you blood.

You would expect the mother to take her down to Newlands with her. As mother. No Sir. Maybe she didn't want to deal with the shame. Those days head teacher was a big thing. Lorita never come back to school. She must be was seven months by the time the mother find out because not long after that she tek een and they rush her to Annatto Bay hospital. Premature birth.

People say the nurses tell them she had a very hard time and from she give birth her eye just cock in one direction. She never come back to her senses. These days they would have a big word for what she had, maybe "Eclampsia" or something. Between that hospital and Bellevue was she that for years and years, till most people must be forget. Not too long ago them send her back to the district, say the community experience will rehabilitate her. Well see her there. She don't rehabilitate.

She live in a house her father did buy up at Point after he retire and move out from the cottage. I don't even know who else in that house.

"What happen to the baby?"

"I hear that her mother give him to a cousin in St. Elizabeth who didn't have any children of her own. If you watch her, old as she is, every now and then she form her hands like she hushing something."

"And what happen to the boy?"

"I hear he did very well, you know. Late developer. The mother send him to England to a brother she had there. I hear that the uncle keep him till him finish school, study for lawyer and come back to Jamaica, but not to this district as you can imagine. Set up practice in Mandeville. Brought back an English wife.

"The old people say: "Woman luck de a dungle; fowl come scratch it up.' Fowl don't ALWAYS come scratch it up though."

MRS. UPTOWN

My dear, I can tell you that woman luck de a dungle and fowl can come scratch it up, for I am a case in point. It is not true that you would have known me or would even have spoken to me when I was the age our granddaughters are now.

These days they are running around picking up men for molesting little girls. They don't know the half. I will tell you my story, for example, in what sounds now like a totally different Karma. We may even have time for me to tell you how I entered this one. I was a single mother. A single teenage mother. You want to hear the story?

He was always waiting at the water's edge sitting in the boat just under the bridge. The first afternoon it was as if he had read my mind. I didn't want to go home. Too much work there. Put on the pot. Peel the bananas. And the yard smelling, all the way to the gate. One or other of my brothers and sisters always seemed to have diarrhoea.

"Come here, Linda. Come sit down here and feel how di boat move."

Later he let me hold on to a rod till I could feel the fish pull. He brought up a snapper, pink with bright eyes.

"Take dis fi yu mother and tell her I send it," he said.

Sometimes when we sat there he would run his fingers along my leg gently, very gently, almost to my thigh. I asked him why and he asked if I didn't like it. Even now the smell of sea salt on the wind brings a pleasurable sensation to me, as if my mind blots out all that came after, when that smell floats in.

The afternoon that was to change my life forever he had asked if I wanted to go to Lime Cay and said we could go and come back in two hours. I figured that was just about as much time as Mama expected me to spend at the library so I said to myself why not, and got in the boat.

Now when I think about it, I wonder how come there were so many questions I didn't ask – about life jackets, for example. Then he could have said, we don't use them and I would, perhaps, have stayed, fearful of sharks and eddies we had heard about as whirlpools, that could pull you under.

Lime Cay was wonderful; water so calm. He said we should swim. But who carries even shorts in a schoolbag when it isn't Phys. Ed. day? Those days I wasn't in the social class that automatically owns a bathing suit. So that was not even a possibility.

Yes we swam. Naked. There was not a body in sight. People who own bathing suits call it skinny dipping. After a while he said he wanted us to try something. It might hurt a little but the sea salt would cut the pain. Now I wonder how he knew it would be my first.

I said to him, "You mean what I think?"

"Mi no know what you tink," he said with his head down. And I saw how ready he was. Vague thoughts from the health science class came to me.

"Yu mad, Maas Ize," I said. "Suppose I get pregnant?" Visions of my ever-pregnant mother flashed before me. But his gentle hands were already upon me and my own hormone system was tuning in. He laughed the kind of laugh that meant I was young and foolish.

"Yu can't get insprigment if we do it in the sea," he said, and pulled me to his swollen self.

I knew why it didn't hurt. The salt water cut the pain. So the sea would prevent me from getting pregnant. The afternoon became overcast. We put back on the dry clothes hanging among the sea grapes. In my mind I knew I would never do it on dry land. Never.

So when the first period didn't come I didn't think anything. I hadn't been too regular anyway. By the time I missed three periods I started to suspect that something was wrong, but not pregnancy. By then we had gone to Lime Cay two or three times and I had started looking forward to it any afternoon that I could make it. I was becoming addicted. We always did it in the sea.

I don't know if you should call it luck but I didn't feel sick one day, and nothing was showing. Even when I reached what must have been six months the uniform (it was a loose tunic with a blouse inside) covered everything. Of course Maas Ize noticed and said something not right but he didn't mention a child. I think I kept hoping it would go away.

One day I was changing and my mother came into the room and there was the belly for all to see. I didn't know it then but she herself was pregnant, on her seventh. So you can imagine her outrage. I didn't go to school that day. She flung away the school bag and with tears in her eyes chased me out of the house, saying I had let her down and that I wouldn't need books where I was going.

"Go fine yu pikni faada," she said. "We kyaa have two belly woman in here." I fled and hid till afternoon when I went to the bridge to find Maas Ize. I had no idea where he lived. Turned out he lived in a yard in Kingston. We took the ferry over and stopped in the market where he bought me some clothes.

I must tell you the women in the yard didn't spare him when he brought me there. Called him all sort of names for taking advantage of somebody girlchild who could be his daughter. But they were kind to me. Showed me how to get registered at Jubilee and how to prepare for the child and everything. I learned on the grapevine that the woman who had left him had said he couldn't have any children.

It was not an easy time. At Jubilee I shared a bed with another teenage mother. In my agony I swore I would never do it again. The women in the yard helped me care for the baby and really you couldn't want a more attentive father than Maas Ize. When he was there. Soon I was pregnant again.

You know, I listen to all the talk about contraceptives and young people. But here I was, a girl living penniless with a man on whom I was totally dependent. After he bought food and clothes for me and a child there wasn't much left. Moreover I don't think the idea of a condom ever came into his head.

When the second child was about three and I was now near twenty he passed the test to go to farm work and left me with the two children and the expectation of the money he would send. Of course he would eventually return. The cheques did come. I started a bank account. He had told me to do that. I lived the same way I was living before and saved what I could. The children went to a little school in an abandoned bus and I put myself together and went to look for work, domestic work.

One day a man was visiting the house where I worked and saw me reading a book. He asked me a whole heap of questions and said I had ambition and he would pay for me to go to evening class. He asked his friend, my employer, to let me off early in the afternoons.

When the lessons (English and Maths) were in full swing he suggested that I work with him Saturdays on a day's work basis so I could make some extra money. A lady in the yard looked at the children for me.

You can guess the rest. First he gave me money so I could rent an extra room. I took two rooms side by side so the children could be in one. But he never really came to me there. Now with him everything was in order. Safe sex every time. Then he started to invite me and the children to spend Sundays there if I would cook Sunday dinner. He was a widow. A lot of his wife's things were around the place still. His children lived abroad and he would visit them sometimes for weeks. I would still go and keep the place clean and the children were exposed to something different.

I don't think his friend, my employer, liked the way things were going. But from one thing to another, with the loneliness and the new habit, he made a decision. He became my first husband. We didn't go to church, though in my heart of hearts I wanted that. But I didn't say a thing. Just thank my lucky stars. Registrar's office and a nice lunch at *Terra Nova*. So my dear, I was always an old man's delight. Jim you see here is the first person I have had whose age is near to mine. And I didn't meet him till I was fifty. In fact, that was before the first husband passed on.

"What became of the children's father?"

"You know I don't know. The cheques suddenly stopped coming about five years after he left. And since I didn't have any status, I wasn't wife, I didn't think I could ask anything. In any case, who would I ask? In those days I had never heard of the Ministry of Labour. I figured he must have died. Now I know more, he may even have just stayed and didn't want to be traced, so he stopped sending. Though to tell you the truth I don't think he would do that. He wasn't that kind of man."

"And your mother?"

"Well she found me. I don't know how. After I got married the first time. By then she had three children needing help with schooling. And my husband was a kind man. In fact they became almost all the family he had, because most of those who knew my story, as you can imagine, sort of cut him off.

"You know, just telling you this story it come to me that is a snapper Maas Ize give me that first afternoon by the water. You know that snapper mean baby?"

"No."

"Yes, red fish is baby if you dream it."

"You too crazy!!!"

"You remember where this conversation started?"

"Yes. 'Young women in crisis.' Isn't that what the tea-ticket said?"

"COME SIT BY MY SIDE (ON MY KNEE) LITTLE DARLING"

They were taking the corner so fast I could hardly keep up with them. They were talking just as fast too. She with the jeans so tight it made her walk kriss. She was saying:

"You would believe the man all want me walk wid him pon street?"

"So why not? What wrong with that? Me walk wid mine, my dear. Anybody who can take me out a my mother one-room shack and give me apartment and food to eat and music to play and don't ask for nothing but..."

"Well me naa walk pon street with no baal head man."

"Shame on you, Deena. Nuttn no wrang wid di man. You know how much woman out there grudge you? You never hear say it's better to be an old man's darling than a young man's delight? My mother always say that."

There was a long pause. Deena had bent to tie the laces of her sneakers; the latest of course. Whoever was coming behind would have seen far more than he/she had bargained for that time of day in that place. The skirt she was wearing was micro, such as I had not seen outside of Brazil.

"What about both?" she asked with a grin as she brought her head up. "You never hear about both?"

"Deena, you no mean seh you a horn di man? Suppose him find out and kill you?"

"I didn't say that. No bada quote mi wrang. In any case, how you so fool? Dem de man no kill. You think him waa finish him days in jail? Im a no no pyaw pyaw man you know. Come off a good table. One of the judge dem, always in the papers: is him brother. And anyway my guy not here. Im de a foreign. I don't see him more than so. I go up two or three time a year and him come down for carnival."

"So what you tell the old man why you go up?"

"Business no. And mi really do business."

"Well yes; there is business and business."

"Let I tell you. Everybody happy. The arrangement not hurting nobody."

I couldn't pretend to need to walk alongside them any more. The pavement disappeared into nothing. I wished a grown man had heard them. It must be nice to be young and desirable. And to know it.

You won't believe, but later that same day, like a nice follow-up to that conversation, I was at a national celebration and saw this young thing dressed, let us say, not for the occasion. Or perhaps I should say dressed like nobody else there and they were addressing her as Mrs. So and So. I recognized the name and somebody introduced me to her. The husband wasn't around. I was more than a little puzzled by the look of her and hoped it didn't show on my face. I commented that though we hadn't met I know that she and her husband had been hosts to friends of mine from another island one time, when I wasn't here. I called the name and said her address to show that I knew what I was talking about.

"Oh, that must be my husband's first wife. We don't live there any more. I am the second wife," she beamed.

Just then the husband appeared and I excused myself. Where was his exercise plan? The paunch was almost touching the company. And what was he doing with that young, slim, badly-dressed girl. How did he face his daughter, who I knew existed? Excuse me, more quietly this time, let me go outside and be sick (again?).

Which reminds me, did you read that story in last month's Red Pages written by a woman just out of anaesthetic after a hysterectomy? Calls itself a "post-uterine mare". Her husband is in a sunken bed and all these (sweet) young things are fluttering around him. All baby mothers of this guy. One is asking for a world tour and the woman (who is his wife) hears herself say, "No, not a world tour. You only have one child for him. There are others of us who have two and three."

Now wonder why she should have such a mare?

Can you imagine working hard to help someone make his fortune and watch him spend it in the evening of his life and yours trying to satisfy the multiple demands of a teenager, almost?

Still, there must be stories we can't tell. There must be something to it, or so many older men wouldn't opt for it regardless. Perhaps it is worth it. Just the thought that at sixty and over you are desirable to one so young.

I am not sure. I don't think it is as simple as that. Let us ask one of those radio talk show hosts to interview some of these people.

BERBICE

"Grandma, where did you get that middle name from? Were you all originally from Berbice?"

"No, we are from Essequibo."

"So why 'Evadney Berbice Mitchell'?"

"And Jonathan Berbice Mitchell and Elizabeth Berbice Mitchell... and in the generation before us, too, you know."

"So you know the reason?"

"Well, I can tell you the story that came down to us but let me warn you it's not nice and if you weren't over twenty-one I couldn't tell you, so is just as well you didn't ask before now."

"Well, I only now find out your full name."

"My grandmother's grandmother, that was slavery time you know, died just after she had baby and apparently she begged them to include Berbice in whatever name they give the child. Say she wanted Massa to feel a pain every time he saw that child or heard the name. I don't know if Massa could feel or did feel any pain. But you know you can't deny the wishes of a dying person. She was the daughter of a house slave, her mother was chief house slave, no. So they say. One evening an old lady took sick and they sent for the mother. Seems like she knew something about medicine, bush medicine of course. Today we would say she was a herbalist.

The old lady lived in a hut quite far from the estate house. Sort of on the border of the estate, for you know when you definitely too old to work they would give you somewhere to live away from working quarters, and you would mind children or whatever down there. So the girl was in the house alone. Mother left her to serve Massa supper. Only Massa was there, for they say the wife had gone to England with the children. And I don't know where the cook or anybody else was. I only know that nobody was in the house.

Well Massa throw her down in the Berbice chair. Look at that one over there. You see the shape? People think the planter brought it here to relax in. That too. But he soon found another use for it. Throw her down in there and had his way with her. Of course since nobody was there nobody couldn't hear her scream. And she did scream. Young girl you know. In any case even if anybody could hear what they could do?

They say she told her mother but the mother couldn't do a single thing. In fact, who knows, maybe he had the mother before, though that didn't come down in the story. Mother give her bush and green pine to drink but it didn't work. She was there getting bigger and bigger.

What rub salt in the wound is that when the mistress came back she was shocked and said it in no uncertain terms because she had loved the young girl and had her as a sort of personal maid. She didn't make fun to tell the girl how disappointed she was that she started off so soon. Told her how after all she was just like all the others and that maybe people of her sort couldn't help themselves. Of course the girl couldn't tell her the truth.

From what I hear the young girl became a different person. Never laugh again from that day, just draw into her shell. Some say she brought on her own death, say she wish for it. Her mother raise the child. She give him the name Berbice as a middle name but she never call him by his first name.

After the funeral and everything the mistress went down to where they lived and took some things for the baby, for she was really a nice lady. They say she fainted when she saw the child and it wasn't just that he wasn't getting black fast enough. It was that you would have to be a fool not to see Massa face print off on him.

I don't know if was because the mother had died like that or what, or whether the mistress had something to do with it, but Massa bought the child out of slavery as soon as he reach a certain age. So when he got his own family, he was a free man.

I suppose his grandmother told him everything and he just decided to keep up the practice. So everybody got the name too. That's how it happen."

"Don't make ghost fool you, is not today man start think that anything him see, him mus get, you know." I am sure you notice the tendency and though I am not one of those who blame everything on slavery, I think it really have to take a little blame. Why I mention slavery is because I was thinking of the GreatGrandNanny of the district I grow up in. They always used to say that everybody in that district related, and you might want to laugh, but is true. Plenty people never believe when all these people say them have the same grandmother for we accustom to believe is only man have plenty children with different partner. Now that big historian go to record office and look it up we find out say that is true that that one lady was great great great grandmother to eight families in the district. Apparently she was a young girl when she come here and get sell to the master of the coffee plantation there.

It seem like all the able-bodied men decide they have to have their time. How else you can explain that she never have more than two children for one man and for most of them is one? Now if it was early up in slavery days you could say they used to bring more men than women on those ships, but according to the records she come sort of late down. Of course, you could say the men got the practice early and continue it till late, even when the statistics wasn't quite so serious.

How the story come down, all of these people talk how them hear that their Grandy was pretty: smooth black skin and heavy engine hair and a kind of rear that move to its own music when she walk. Nearly every year she had a baby. Seem like nearly every year somebody different walk with her. I suppose that was before jealousy create here. And as far as the plantation

108

and the boss man go, woman make to have baby so more and more slave would born. When you find one that breed well – 'low her. Breed well mean didn't get too sick to work. From what I hear Madru would work up to the day before she have baby. And she didn't have no long labour. Not like some of them.

People say that even Bakra didn't allow himself to get leave out, but that she did say long time, "Mi no want no malata pikny." Of course, she couldn't prevent him from holding her down any time him feel like. In fact I hear that him use to position himself at a certain angle to look out the greathouse window in the evening when she going home. Used to call her "my Hottentot Queen". But she always keep a shut-pan with green-pine grater and dry and she would steep it in boiling water. Like tea. Strong. And she would drink that after every time him go to her.

Yes, she was a good breeder but she set up her own standards and she figure out how to exercise her choice.

ON MY WAY TO SOMEWHERE, OF COURSE

MIAMI AIRPORT

(for Evelyn)

The little sign, the stick-woman with her skirt, indicated that this was the ladies loo. I pushed the door. It wouldn't give. I pushed more firmly for I had to go. And this was not the corridor with lines of signs gates 1, 3, 5 or 2, 4, 6, etc. if-you-miss-one-restroom-there-will-be-another. This was THE gate and this one washroom that final chance before you board.

Eventually the door gave, but slowly. I could feel things moving behind it. I squeezed myself in and pulled my slim hand-luggage with me. There was barely space. The room was so full of packages you couldn't see the door to the toilet. I started to reverse. I wasn't sure I could handle this. But a voice of welcome sounded, "Come in… Come in," and a quick assessment told me I had to stay before they decided to tell me who I thought I was not to want to be in that place with them.

"This one very small," the voice continued. "They usually larger than this." I tried to smile and not to stare.

To my left was a huge and naked breast and on its left another only slightly smaller. Their owner was paying no attention to them but was wiping her armpit with a small rag. I followed the movement of her hand and discovered that a wash basin, presumably for everybody's use, was in that direction.

A woman and child squeezed in behind me and I indicated that the child should go first. That mother will never know that inquisitiveness as much as courtesy prompted my action. I had to see what else there was. Also the urgency had left me when the truth of the location showed itself.

Other women, at different stages of undress, were quietly

fixing themselves amid boxes, some with strange labels like "Quartz Clock" and others with no label at all. The intermittent chatter was enough to make me glean that it was the end of a three-day shopping expedition.

The little girl emerged. So finally I went through the door into the toilet fighting the shame that I didn't trust the sisters enough to leave my luggage outside beside their own so hardearned loads.

Out again I needed to wash my hands and said so in the friendliest voice I could muster.

"Pass, pass," says the bather.

The breasts are still out there. Now I can see the black halfslip complete with slit at the side. Something must be showing on my face for she offers: "The skirt fall down."

I washed my hands and took a last peek at the breasts. Especially the larger one. I remembered another breast splayed all over the TV screen one night I visited my ex entertaining friends in his nest. Only, that breast was white. I wondered why the skirt had fallen down. There was so much hip to support it. I had heard her telling her friends she would start a diet the next week. She hadn't started it before she travelled because of how frequently it would cause her to want to use the loo. She didn't put it quite like that.

I had long settled in my new chair, having moved from beside the brother flossing his teeth, when a well-clad lady, neatly zippered in, entered the departure lounge. There was nothing to relate her to the breasts I had left untended in the washroom. Nothing but the face. The kindly face which I had managed to take in amidst all that flesh and luggage.

What do they know of journeys who only journeys know?

The woman beside me was leaning on the handle of her carry-on case. Her sunglasses were stuck on the crown of a head covered with hair standing on end. I hadn't seen a wig like that before. Every now and then she took a sip from the bottle of water she was carrying. I wondered whether we all had simply been walking around dehydrated before the Americans announced that this was a healthy habit.

Easily visible from where we were sitting was an older woman with a small child leaning against her. Both my neighbour and I turned as the woman suddenly started to talk as if oblivious of the fact that she was addressing us:

"The smaddy who coming for you better come before Monday. I am your grandmother. I say that but I have my life to live. I try. God know I try."

The mean-faced older woman was talking to (or at) the meekest looking three-year-old you have ever seen. The little girl looked up at her with eyes at once sad and thoughtful, then held her head down and gazed at the floor. I didn't think she understood much of what the woman said but she must have caught the emotion.

"You vex with you Granny? Don't vex."

The little girl managed a slight smile. I thought of my own three-year-old granddaughter – strong willed, opinionated. Loved. Indulged even. One foot and a half high and defiant in the presence of an angry father standing six foot four. I recognize it as the kind of fearlessness that takes people confidently through an uncompromising world. I thought of my grandson who at two would climb to the top of the burglar bars and yell: "Save me, save me!" completely confident that someone would.

I wondered where the granddaughter of this woman would get the confidence to compete eventually with those and others like them in the corridors of the world. She who had heard her grandmother say clearly that she was anxious to be rid of her. She understood the emotion already. The words would stay with her and make sense later. Jackass say the world no level. It is true. In another culture they call the world the playing field.

The grandmother's voice piped up again and drew me from my reverie.

"Don't vex with you Granny, you hear. But you Granny tired."

She hugged the child hard, tears clouding her eyes.

I didn't know her story but I could easily imagine it. I looked at her again and no longer saw a mean-faced old woman. I simply saw a tired, ageing woman with a painful story. I knew many like her. Hadn't she given her all, beat out her soul-case to raise her own children, possibly without a father? She said she was tired. Hadn't she looked forward to these years to treat herself well, at least to have no responsibility?

But she was taking down from New York a grandchild she was almost sure would be left with her. She had flattered herself that they had sent the ticket so she could have a holiday. Why was she so gullible? The truth became clear soon enough. How many other grandchildren had been left with her for two or three years at a time?

Who was the other person who was slated to relieve her? Who was the "smaddy" to whom she referred? The father's sister? Another grandmother like herself? She was obviously not confident that the person would materialize.

My eyes made four with the woman sipping the water. She was holding her head down. The tissue she moved along her cheeks was stained black with tears mixed with mascara.

I looked at the writing pad in my hand and read what I had written when I first saw her enter the departure lounge:

> *Dear Lorna*
> *You have already written about Bella, so I don't need*

to write about this lady of exquisitely reined-in flesh held in place by the shortest skirt you have ever seen; nor do I have to mention some of the flesh escaping under the skimpy top and hanging out over the waist like a soft crag; nor yet about the brassiere straps competing with the top for space along the shoulder (and winning); about her hair standing on end in a revised version of senseh fowl and finally about the string of cowrie beads at her neck shouting: "I am me and I am proud. Who don't like it bite it." .

I ran my pencil through it. I felt a little ashamed. Now she was simply a fellow traveller. Another woman. With compassion.

COINCIDENCE
(AT ST. MAARTEN AIRPORT)

The heart-shaped cargo earrings had a bar across which read "Love". I thought her ears bearing the weight might wish to write "Hate".

The little girl at her side wore an ankle-length dress. Satin trimmed with lace. There were frills from chest to hem with a brief relief at the waist. Her hair and the extensions were in twists; about thirty of them and there were beads hanging from each twist. Somehow it seemed a sin to put such a great weight on a little child's head.

The woman was wearing leather boots, ruffled, rather like the brake shoes the mechanic leaves to show you he did exchange your old ones for new. It seems that boots no longer have to do with snow and cold (but then cowboy boots never did). Perhaps it was always a case of fashion first.

The man who hugged her and kissed the little girl where the sign said "Passengers Only" was tall and good-looking. He wasn't wearing any heavy jewellery, just a simple gold chain with a cross at his neck.

She was going to be on my flight. Going back home to Jamaica. She had decided to take the child on this shopping run. She had never taken her before. Not to Panama. Not to Curaçao. She liked St. Maarten. She had started to prefer it to Panama and Curaçao.

People hear about a Dutch Island and think there might be a language problem for English-speaking Caribbean people. But Jamaican higglers faced Papiamento, Dutch and Spanish in Curaçao fearlessly long ago. In any case, Dutch on the streets of St. Maarten is as scarce as money in Jamaica.

The woman had extra good reason to make it St. Maarten now. She had brought the child with her for a little holiday, a few

118

extra days after the shopping. It was more than that. She had promised to bring her to meet her new sweet St. Maarten man who really came from St. Croix, USVI. He with the US Green card and a bright road over his shoulder. She was beginning to feel he was OK and that maybe they could start something, but he had to like the child. Or else she wasn't playing. She wasn't going to be like any of these women who sacrifice child for man. This was not a come-by-chance-child. This child father would still be with her now if that back hoe hadn't scooped him up. And his brothers still help with the child.

From what she was telling her friend Ruby (and me uninvited) the meeting had gone well. The little girl took to him and he to her. Ruby was talking up the little girl.

"You like St. Maarten?"

"Yes."

"Yes who?" the mother asked.

"Yes, Miss Ruby."

"You would live here?"

"I want to go to my same school so I can't leave Jamaica."

"You would come for holidays though?"

"Yes, Miss Ruby."

"Ruby, it don't reach thereso yet you know," the mother said. Then putting on a shy little-girl look asked, "How you like my earrings?" Ruby said they were nice and smiled in a way which meant she understood that they were a gift from the man.

I was disappointed. I liked the look of the man. I didn't want to know that he had bought those ugly earrings. But she was obviously very pleased with them. I started to hope he did not have a wife somewhere. My head was still full of all that the taximan had told me about the behaviour of Jamaican women and Dominican women in St. Maarten. He spoke of men leaving their wives or starting parallel and preferred families right before their eyes. Especially with the Dominican women who would bear nice brown-skin children.

"I see with me own two eyes man go look school fi di Dominican woman pikni dem and lef fi him own naa gaa no school. Is long time this going on. My own faada lef wi an mi mother fi one a dem. But I don't bear dem no grudge and I still treat fi her children like mi brother and sister."

So I asked him what the Jamaican women had to offer since they usually had no brown-skin babies to give. In any case, I couldn't understand why he was placing the blame on the women. (Of course, I knew. After all I had heard *Genesis* read in church over and over and I knew that Adam was forever blameless.)

I asked him whether he didn't think the men should take some of the blame. Somehow he managed not to hear that question. He had spoken with such passionate anger about the Jamaicans that I suspected first-hand experience. I repeated the original question. He paused for a while. A sheepish grin came over his face:

"Dem know how fi mek man feel good, Miss. You see our women know how to cook and keep the house clean and look after the children, but dem don't make the man feel good."

I was a little embarrassed as he described for me the extra dimension Jamaican women brought to bedroom interaction, while making disparaging comments about the local women. But I said nothing beyond my grunted "mhmm".

They called the flight. The woman got on with Ruby and the little girl and me. The good-looking man from foreign had given her a tight hug and got a kiss from the little girl.

You will not believe this but TWO years later I had a meeting in Anguilla and took the advice of a friend to fly to St. Maarten and cross on the ferry (those were the days when Jamaicans didn't need a visa to go to Anguilla). It was Norman Manley Airport, Kingston this time, and it was the end of August. Same woman. Same child. Inches taller. Fewer baubles in her hair. Extensions now on the hair of both Mother and child except that the mother's were orange. There was no Ruby with them.

Migration… I thought. My pet peeve… Again. I started to empathize with the now-not-so-little-girl. She would go to school in St. Maarten. New friends; new school system; new language. Dutch was still the language of instruction though the Education people were fighting desperately for a novel arrangement which would allow English to replace it in those islands where the popular language was overwhelmingly English or an English Creole. I felt sorry for the child but consoled myself with the thought that if her mother had been a diplomat it would be the same story at a different level.

There was no customs to go through. The good-looking man was already at the exit door. Smiling. I wondered then why I was worrying about the child. Why didn't I just feel glad for the woman. She in a relationship that had survived two years. Going to a new start, new man, new location. She needed my blessing.

ISLAND TRAVEL

On my way from Puerto Rico to some islands farther south, American Eagle books me on its own planes, but taking me out of St. Vincent it uses Helen Air for the leg St. Lucia to Dominica. Why oh why, I plead with the travel agent, must I spend a whole day in the airport in St. Lucia from 8:30 am to 5 pm to make the connection.

"Is there no other flight?"

I am on a tight schedule and I tell her this but she says it can't be helped. OK so I have to waste a whole day in the airport.

I am thinking that this is not good. But I am no stranger to St. Lucia so I make a telephone call or two. The morning I arrive a car collects me and whisks me off to a friend's house to spend the morning gorging on wonderful food (more brunch than breakfast) and laughing with old and new friends. Not for long enough though. They all have to go to the opening of a flower show in the south of the island and so deposit me at the airport at a quarter to one. What can I do for the next four hours beside read? Maybe LIAT, with all its impossible stops, was worth a try.

I go to the Helen Air desk and ask if they can help me; try to get me on a flight on another airline etc. etc. The agent looks at me curiously and says, "Madam the flight to Dominica left at 12:30."

Me: (astonished) "What? American Eagle told me 5 pm Here's the ticket."

She: "That flight stopped since December (this was March), and LIAT is overbooked. So tomorrow at 12:30 eh! I'll find you a nice cheap hotel."

While I contemplate the prospect of calling to reschedule

the interviews set up so many months before, she calls a hotel. It has room and yes it is cheap. She books a room for me.

"Can you call a taxi for me?"

"No. Is within walking distance. Go to the end of this road, right here take a sharp left at the traffic lights and you are immediately at the gate. Climb some steps and you are there."

I slung my little travel bag over my shoulder and set out.

I am a Caribbean woman. I live with "soon come" and "round the corner" and "ef you walk fast yu wi ketch", so why was I not even slightly suspicious of the distance the kind lady described?

I walked and walked. The sun felt hotter and hotter. The road got dustier and dustier. I passed first one then two hotels recessed with grassy lawns on either side of entrance paths; grass that made you feel cool just to look at it. They had no steps. I soldiered on. I reached the traffic lights and looked up. There at the top of twenty steps (at least) was the bright sign of the hotel whose card I had in my hand; the place where she had kindly booked me a room.

I thought about the term "walking distance" again. Walking distance for whom? A young soldier perhaps. Did I look that fit to her? She never had to walk to that hotel. After all, she was never a visitor to St. Lucia and in all likelihood she always drove or was driven home. When you are in a car distances look short. I veered between that explanation and the cultural one: "round the corner".

Sweat was poring over me. But worse than sweat was the shower of self-pity that covered me. I felt poor in every sense. Unfortunate. Obviously not well-heeled. That one obvious enough for the travel clerk to figure out what hotel I could afford.

I gathered up the puny strength I had left and climbed the steps. I reached the front desk and flopped down in a settee, there shouting my name to the man at the desk.

"Yes," he said. "You have a reservation?"

He turned to get the form for me to fill out. I took a granola bar from my bag and started to chew on it. I needed that. I stood to sign the form, handed the man my credit card and eventually got a key. He directed me to my room. Up two flights. The horror in my eyes was visible.

"Something wrong?" he asked.

I begged him to give me a different room. On the floor we were on if at all possible. I couldn't climb two flights after what I had just gone through. The one other room available was one flight up. It was more expensive. I took it with glee and paid the extra from my wallet.

The man, who seemed to be the proprietor, showed me to the room, turned on the ceiling fan and indicated a kitchenette. On the same floor! I could see that there was a kettle there. I thanked him. He hesitated and started asking me questions about myself: where I was from? What I was doing in St. Lucia? etc. etc. I answered in monosyllables. He said he had worked many years in England. I thought I had guessed that from a little something in his accent. I tried to smile, told him I was extremely tired and asked to be excused. I threw my bag on the bed and took a package (tea and milk) from the pocket on the side.

I went to the kitchenette and plugged in the kettle. Call me colonial if you wish. If the British hadn't introduced me to tea the Chinese would have eventually. I made the best cup of tea I have ever had.

I called front desk, gave the man my flight number for the next day and asked him to book me a taxi to the airport.

WHAT IS FI YU (MIAMI AIRPORT II)

They from the outer culture call it Fate. We from inside don't deal with abstractions. We say "what is fi you can't be unfiyu", which translates to a sort of English: "What is yours cannot be unyours."

It wasn't the thirteenth of any month. It was ten days beyond it. The 23rd. of August. And there I was sitting in Miami Airport (again?) full four hours before my flight would leave, if it did leave, with the TV threatening a hurricane packing winds three hundred miles per hour through voices that tried to veil their hysteria in so many different ways.

Where I come from you have to pass through Miami to go to places that are nearer to you than Miami: Puerto Rico, Nassau, Mexico, Belize. Something to do with airlines and how much money they need to make. And I was coming from Belize. I had been scheduled to do a Belize/Jamaica trip in one day. But the thought of Kingston, especially the airport road near midnight, did not thrill me. It wasn't a month yet since Reverend Somebody on that same road did not make it to the airport, ending up of all places in a pit latrine in Trench Town. And nobody to give any explanation. Elaine the wise had agreed with me that I had no business on that road so late.

So I changed my booking, with American Airlines cooperating, and decided to overnight in Miami and leave the next afternoon, the 23rd. Just as well for I had some unfinished business with my friend Alfred. He owed me a shrimp biryani.

I had paid no attention to the TV in Belize City. They were preparing for a wedding reception upstairs in *The Orchid* where I was staying. I was too taken with feeling powerful, as the sounds from Jamaica, Bob Marley and all that, reassured me that we had colonized the region musically, to bother to listen to radio or watch TV. I heard nothing when I got to Miami Airport. My head was still light as I stepped out into the Miami air that many hours later. And I was smiling at the thought of not having to run to make a connection – which is what I usually have to do in Miami airport.

I called Alfred and went downstairs to wait as usual, on the curb where travellers wait for rides coming to collect them. It would take him twenty minutes to get to me. I enjoyed looking at the world. All kinds of people drive up there on the curb outside Miami Airport.

Alfred came, bringing a friend. The friend was a weather man and between them, while trying not to frighten me, they managed to frighten me so much that I didn't sleep a wink that night.

Next day as the radio announced shelters and kept everyone in touch with which avenues would be closed I thought I better get out of South West and into the airport building.

I gave thanks for "hand luggage only". There were long lines of people trying to check in. I walked over hordes of those whose planes already said they wouldn't go, huddled for sleep for a number of days they couldn't then predict.

Air Jamaica was leaving from an international terminal so I was sharing waiting space with whites and the odd top-drawer black. You know the kind. They wear Bally shoes and Saville Row or pseudo-Saville Row suits and are intransit from some world to Brussels or Geneva on some EEC intent or other

I kept phoning Alfred every hour on the hour. He was loading cars, his and his friends', on to the roof. I was trying not to panic further. A young man heading home to Peru rushed in from LA and made it breathless to the gate to hear his plane would not be going. He didn't have a cent in his pocket. After all he was going home. Some decent son's father put his hand on his shoulder and I knew he would be OK if not safe.

What is fi yu canNOT be unfiyu. I left on the last flight out of Miami. I was going to be out there on the airport road late after all. Suddenly I wasn't worrying about sharing the fate of Reverend Somebody. I was going to be glad to be there at all.

BETTER TALES

GRACE

Just enough rain to cool down the place and it stopped in time. Graduation was out there on the lawn in front of the Undercroft, not in any choky "alternative location". And me sitting there awestruck as I always am in that place, thinking that there is definitely no sight more beautiful than the Mona campus at night. The mountains: blue mixed with grey in varying proportions, one set resting on the other till the last one touching the sky points to clouds changing shape and scampering by. So often when I see it I think of Wordsworth and how if he were alive and I had the money I would send him a ticket and we would never hear anything more about how fair the sight from Westminster Bridge is/was.

Then as dusk descended, the procession in the half light looked so orderly and truly majestic. Paraphernalia of all different styles. Of course the various "hats" were sort of comical, making most of the men look, from the neck up, as if they were in a play or some carnival band. I have this friend who returned home to Trinidad after a Ph.D in England and the only thing customs charged him for was the cap and gown. Say is Carnival costume. They right.

People think of the ceremony as long and boring. Perhaps. But this one was neither long nor boring. To me. One of the Honorary Graduands was Jimmy Cliff and when he came to get his scroll the perfect sound system belted out him singing "Many Rivers to Cross". Then at some point, without a break, the University Singers took over (like the smooth passing of a baton in a relay). Ever heard such sweet music? I wasn't bored. I wasn't tired. I was intoxicated…

Eventually the long strings of names came. I like names you know. Have always been fascinated with names. Not quite as many quaint ones as in the early days when Mona was the only campus and everybody from everywhere in the Caribbean graduated from there.

"Mr. Chancellor, I present…" I wonder how Mr. Chancellor hand not tired shaking all those hands. Medicine was last. And my girl name near the end.

"Angela Grace Liverpool!" She walked up proudly and smiled her sweet and gracious smile. I clapped and her whole class was clapping. I don't know what happened after that. How could I have guessed that this was how it would go. Cold sweat was washing me.

"You alright?" That was Marva, my forever friend and bulwark.

"Yes man," I replied without conviction. Then I could feel the bay rum (without which she never moved) on her handkerchief on my forehead as I left the campus completely… and I was back in St. Catherine that cool cool morning this child was given to me.

I had been on the road. Trying to reach Jubilee Town early. I needed to check upon a project there. I thought I could wait till I reached, but nature is a funny thing. Has its own mind. I would have to stop. I couldn't keep it any longer. If I were a man I could find a tree or simply turn my back. If I were a dog a lamppost, but no, it was me – and I was not wearing a loose skirt. The irony of the pants suit. Takes more than that to make you a man… So I parked and walked towards the house I knew no one had lived in since Miss Gatha's death. There was a pit latrine there. I took some tissue from its place near the steering wheel and some old newspaper and ran up the hill. I needed both. Just as I was pulling up my pants I heard "Jingle Bells" being played on a tape-recorder. Where was the sound coming from? I certainly hadn't seen anyone and the morning silence had been palpable before the sound began. It was coming from inside the pit. I lifted the lid again and could feel my eyes popping out of my head. There was a baby there resting on a large Christmas card which was cheerfully playing "Jingle bells". The baby must have turned and rested on the card suddenly and the mechanism had tripped in. So the baby must be alive.

I rushed to the car for the blanket that stays in the trunk. The hot pee I sent down must have shocked the child into activity. Perhaps she had been sleeping. I ran back up the slight slope trying hard to concentrate. My hands were shaking as I picked up the tiny person and wrapped her in the blanket. She wasn't really that dirty. The latrine had not been much in use. She was surely alive and started to squirm a little. But she didn't cry. I was too frightened to wonder about that or to indulge any emotion. I had to think quickly. I did have a flask with hot water and a spoon and some milk powder in the car. My mother's instruction never to travel without food…

I rested the little bundle on the floor. She must be drugged. This can't be natural behaviour. Why wasn't she crying? I rushed back to the car and took the basket from the trunk. The latrine did not face the road. In any case I had not seen a soul in what seemed to me like hours.

I ladled drops of warm milk into the tiny mouth. One thing was certain; I wasn't going to any police for them to take this child and put her into any home for abandoned children. From that moment forward she would no longer be abandoned. She swallowed a little milk and closed her eyes. She fell asleep immediately.

Please God, I prayed, don't let her die.

If anybody had noticed me they would have thought I was mad. I was talking all the time. To God. Thanking Him out loud over and over, confident that he was hearing.

I drove like Jehu to Jubilee where Marva was matron. Going to Jubilee Town and the project no longer seemed urgent. I knew I could trust Marva. I gave the porter a note and soon she came rushing out. I told her the story and only then I started to cry. Yes, she would take her into the hospital and keep her for me till I had organized my thing. There wasn't a problem. Nobody would even notice one additional abandoned baby. I told her it wouldn't take me more than a week. She said she would get the doctors to do all the necessary tests for me. Contacts she certainly had.

I had wanted a child so badly; how many ways I had thought about to get one. I had convinced myself it wasn't a selfish wish;

nothing about wanting a biological experience (though that would have been nice) but more the pleasure of giving the same kind of affection that I had been given to somebody on a constant basis, in a total way. Friends had made the adoption process sound daunting. I had wanted a newborn. This one was almost new. God had sent her. But so suddenly and without my praying about it recently! I knew then that He never forgets. There was so much I had to work out to accommodate her in my life now. I knew better than to think that we always get a chance to decide what happens in our lives and when.

Her life would begin at Jubilee. Abandoned there. Nobody would ever know the toilet business. This child would one day ask questions because she would surely be told she was adopted. No two schools about that. It wouldn't sound good to say she was found in a latrine. Jubilee was a word that sounded victory and celebration anyway. It would do. And it wasn't a total lie. And I had been on my way to Jubilee Town. Fancy that.

Marva had kept squeezing my hand from time to time as if to be sure I was alive. I was alert enough to squeeze back meaning I was OK. She was the proud godmother. As much the mother as I was. But she was braver. Or she felt one of us had to be. This time she shook my shoulder hard. I came back to the present and heard my girl's voice echoing out over the campus. She was giving the Valedictorian's speech. Flawlessly. No surprises here. She hadn't told me she was valedictorian. This was a new thing at graduation anyway. Maybe they hadn't given her much notice. It ended and everybody was clapping.

And I was thinking back to her years through school, through university and to all the other speeches she had made: prep school, high school graduation. And besides, there wasn't anything she hadn't taken part in at school. Even here at university she had been brilliant in her class "smoker". Stuffed up back and front playing matron in one of the skits. (I don't know where the name "Smoker" comes from.) After her year I made sure I got tickets every year. It never ceased to surprise me that medics did so well in the finer things. And I had watched the smoker as an institution grow to become one of the most popular dramatic events on the campus.

Then there had been track and tennis at high school, after track and ballet at prep. school. And she had stayed with the ballet at the School of Dance certainly to the end of high school. I had been truly blessed. Even the single-mother business that I thought about during the early days had not been a problem at all. Between friends and a vast extended family there were enough willing surrogate fathers around. One of them had laughed and said, "I woulda wear jacket fi that one."

I always remember a friend of mine saying he grew up with his mother and brother and did not know how to handle adult quarrels. So when his wife started up he would just crawl into his shell. She was brought up in a nuclear family which had to deal with all the attempts her father made to extend it. I myself had tried the marriage thing early in life. It hadn't worked. Of course, there had been no children but I was pretty sure it would have been an even greater challenge sharing child-rearing with someone as opinionated as my ex than it could ever be on my own. No, I am not making a case for single parenthood. I still think the nuclear family is best. When it works.

Of course, I had been lucky. All my prayers had been heard upstairs. The stories my friends told! The horrors parents shared with me! Their disappointment and the shame when the principal called them in. Girls putting on uniforms, leaving home and not reaching school is not a new thing. My girl spared me all such thrills. And on parents' days the teachers were always happy to see me. You know how they like children with good grades and they extend the goodwill to the parents.

Of course there had been moments when I felt shaky and surprisingly alone. After High School, for example, she came to say she was getting engaged. Now she had been seeing this young man for a year or two. Quite a polite young man but she knew I didn't really approve. First she was young. Then I wasn't sure where he was coming from – his background.

This Jamaica must be the most class-ridden little society on earth, but why? I hadn't said anything because she would definitely have shouted "prejudice" and I might have lost her forever. I couldn't share this one with friends because I was ashamed to admit how much I was like all the others. I who had held forth so often on the subject of all these sons and daughters of African slaves and British thugs pretending that they had come from somewhere.

On weekends he assisted in his uncle's cabinet shop. Of course, nothing was wrong with that. But when she talked about engagement as soon as she finished sixth form I was alarmed. I had thought the affair would run its course and disappear. She had applied to enter medical school and stood a good chance of getting in if Sister's word was anything to go by. She was slated to get As in the four A level subjects she was sitting.

"David and I know our minds."

"But you are a child and he is little more than one."

"People mature at different ages, Mom."

"You know anything about him except that his uncle own that shop? In fact you don't even know if he owns it."

She paused, a frown darkening her face.

"He don't know anything about me either except that you are my mother."

She had read my mind and shamed me. I suggested weakly that I would just prefer if she reached a little further on in life first. In any case she was from MY family. I had to give in and confess to the trusty Marva. She handled that one. Apparently she didn't stop seeing him but I didn't hear any more talk about engagement.

And now she was engaged. To the same young man. He had gone up to the US of A soon after she entered university. The first two summers she went "up" to earn some money in a wonderful scheme called Youth Unlimited which found jobs for students and vouched for their return home and their exit out of Uncle Sam's country.

After second MB there were no more summers but there always seemed to be a little break and she always seemed to have saved up her money. Or so she claimed. My guess was that he worked at least two jobs while he was studying. From time to time I got what bits of information she would give me.

First he did accounts and that allowed him to get jobs that paid well. Then he did law.

He said he had come home to do the required six months at Norman Manley to allow him to practise in the Caribbean. She would be doing her internship at KPH. I felt suitably humble. She would be living at home so I would have my chance to be nice to him.

The variegated colours on the platform were shifting as the rows of academics began to move. On the ground the tall woman with the mace was walking as if she was carrying the cross in a procession in church. They were all beautiful again.

The lights marked out New Castle on the hills in the distance. The mountains high above had become mere shadows. And above them were stars.

SMILE (GOD LOVES YOU)

I remember it clear clear like is yesterday the evening the car drive up and the brown lady, smiling with the broad hips, stop at our gate. The sun was setting bright yellow like when storm going to come. She walk up the hill and we stop playing ring ding and run to call Mama. Mama come out the kitchen dripping with sweat and smile at the lady. They walk across the yard to the house and we go on playing ring ding, all the while wondering what a lady like that want with Mama.

After a while Mama come to the door and call me. And dry dry so she just say:

"Ayesha, this is Miss Jonas. You going to live with her. She want a little girl who can jump round."

I was seven. Just ready to leave Miss Jo-Ann basic school where the others drop me off on their way to big school every morning. When school open again I would at last be going to big school. It take me a little time to understand what my mother saying. She go inside and bring out a cardboard box and give it to the lady. I glimpse my pink dress on the top and I wondering how come I don't even see when she packing the box nor notice that she wash all my clothes.

"How long a going for?" I ask her.

"You going to stay all the time, but she will bring you to look for us now and then. No true, Miss Pat?"

"Of course, Miss Gloria."

I follow the two of them into the hall.

I could just barely see Keisha and Jasmine and my friend Danaira through the half-open door. They come up quietly and stand behind it. My sisters stand up there staring. They surprise just like me.

My mother push the door and come out. Miss Patricia Jonas follow her.

"Ayesha going to live with this lady," my mother tell them. "She want a little girl."

The lady put her arms around my shoulders. I pull away a little and my sisters form a circle around me. I remember the floral dress I have on and the rubber slippers I wear to school sometimes.

"Then is so she going?" Keisha ask when she find her tongue. Nakeisha three years older than me and facety.

"Yes man, when she go she will bathe and change her clothes. I don't want night to catch us," Miss Jonas say talking like she know us long time.

All of them follow me to the car. Crying. I too shock to cry. My face set up and I feel like it could never laugh again. I vex with my mother. I grudge my sisters who get to stay. I feel like the God who I say my prayers to every night betray me.

Miss Jonas talking all the time, trying to sweet me up telling me how I going to like her house. When we reach she show me my room and the bathroom. She give me a towel and tell me to bathe and put on some clean things from the box while she warm up some supper for us. She smile and touch my chin like how big people always doing to children and goat kid.

Me and she alone at the table. The supper look more like dinner to me. Rice and peas and plenty slice of meat. It was beef. I get four piece. I never get so much meat in my life. At home we call it "watchman", sitting down on the pile of rice or swimming in the gravy at the side of the plate. And fry plantain. Well the fry plantain make me feel better than anything else in the place. They cut in little round pieces and I take six.

The supper always big in this house. Miss Jonas never give porridge or johnny cake. I miss the johnny cake though. Some children call them roast dumpling but Mama always say is johnny cake. She used to make them on a flat thing she call toaster. It look like some circles join on to one another with a handle to hold so it won't burn you. Every circle take one johnny cake. She put it over live coal in the clay stove. Not bright red coal, sort of ashy, and they bake slow slow. Then she cut them open and put a little margarine. Sometimes nothing. That and your mug of mint or fevergrass for supper.

The new school was near to Miss Jonas house. I could see the top from her gate. So I didn't have any long walk to go to school. The first day Miss Jonas go with me to register me. I was really frighten but by the next day I get over it. One good thing was that everybody new to big school and almost everybody live near. This big school was bigger than the one my sister and her friends go to. The one I was to go to. My uniform was a green plaid tunic with a white blouse. If I did stay at home I would be wearing a brown tunic with a yellow blouse. I get five white blouse and two tunic. Miss Jonas say that washing taking place only one time a week and I have to be clean everyday. I remember Keisha with her two yellow blouse always washing in the evening and hoping rain don't fall to prevent the one she wash from drying.

Every Saturday night I cry myself to sleep. Everybody at home would be in the kitchen helping grate potato and coconut to make the pudding Mama make every Saturday night so we could have it for supper Sunday evening. When it just bake she give all who help a little piece. Hot. That special. Sunday evening it cold and the gumption settle on the top. Mama say that is because of the coconut milk. It still nice but different.

Sunday I know Mama and the children gone to church. I have to go to church with Miss Jonas. She say nobody not living in her house and don't go to church.

But her church don't feel like church. The singing dead. No tambourine not shaking. Nobody moving. Most of the time is the parson alone talking and nobody answering him. When they do answer they just say one or two little words. Sometimes the parson sing the prayers but is a kind of singing that you not sure is really a song; sort of like how a ram goat bawl when him know him going to bawl whole night till them let him go. Not too loud, not too soft and sort of trembly. So I just sit down and sleep. Only one time in the whole service you see any action. That time everybody stand up and start walking around telling one another, "Peace be with you." I usually don't get up. My face must be look vex for most of them pass me over after they try once or twice and see it. But this one lady always force up herself on me and tell me "Smile. God loves you." She don't have to tell me God loves me. I hear that all the time at my church but from the day Miss Jonas take me a start doubt him. I never understand why is me she take. And I never understand why Mama agree to give me away.

I don't want you to get the feeling that Miss Jonas don't treat me good or anything like that, you know. I couldn't want a nicer lady. And she don't give me too much work to do. I have to keep my room clean, wash my underwear and socks (she make me wear socks to church) and on the days when the helper don't come I sweep out the living room and the dining room. Sometimes she come home late. She show me how to set the table and warm up my supper in the little oven. The helper lady cook enough food when she come to give us enough to just warm up on the days when she don't come. I have to set the table for the two of us and sit down and eat mine. When is me alone I eat with a spoon but when she is there I have to try with the knife and fork. Make me eat very slow. And she tell me to chew everything thirty-two times. Even rice. I laugh in my mind because she couldn't eat her own food and keep up with counting how many times I chew. She say one day when I get my big job and have to eat with high people I will thank her for making me eat with knife and fork and chew decent. I never bother to tell her that I see high people on her same TV eating with fork alone and sometimes with their hand.

When Easter holidays come Miss Jonas ask me if I want to spend a weekend at home. I was so happy me heart start beat hard hard. School close Wednesday. She take me down Thursday evening and say she coming for me Easter Monday because we have a fair to go to. The little Easter at home; the little change was wonderful. Everybody glad to see me. Keisha hug me up so tight a think me tripe would squeeze out. When I look at all of them water come to me eye. Miss Jonas drive off and is just as if I never leave. After that, every holiday I get a little chance to go home.

You can get used to things. And in a way because Miss Jonas treat me good I could get through the days. But I never stop wanting to know why Mama give one of us away and why me. I never confront her with the question. I understand that she poor. And she say I bright and could make use of the chance. And Miss Jonas say she want a little girl who could jump roun and Mama always say that about me, "Ayesha, carry dis down a bridge for me. Come back quick and sweep out the kitchen when you come. Me know you can jump roun." When I go there in the holiday the same Mama make much of me and ask me to do this and that.

Time fly. Common Entrance come. First time I take it I pass for Knox College. Keisha take it two times but she only pass for All-Age School. So maybe I really bright. That is what my teacher tell Miss Jonas. Or maybe my teacher just better. I don't know. Miss Jonas make sure I do my home work and coming near on to Common Entrance she buy practice books and take me through them every week. Mama couldn't do that for Keisha. Mama don't have no big education.

The church thing still botheration though. I use to really hate Miss Jonas church. And I have to go every Sunday unless I really sick. And the same woman I talk about keep on giving me the peace although I don't answer and she keep on saying, "Smile, God Loves You."

One Thursday evening I come home early from school. Miss Jonas didn't come home yet. I was feeling very lonely. Where she live not near to anybody else house so after you play at school you don't have anybody to play with at home. I sit down with me hand at me jaw singing this little Sankey from my mother church. My grandmother used to like it. That's my mother mother. Used to love me you see. I always feel that if she was alive Mama couldn't give away any of us. I was sitting down propping up sorrow singing her song "Have ye trials and temptations…" As a finish the line I hear clear as day Granny singing "Is there trouble anywhere?" Then she stop and say, "Ayesha you have to get out of this frowning or else dem going to mark you with it. Now you into high school. Nobody not going to put up with it."

I wasn't sleeping. I wasn't dreaming. So she didn't dream me. She come and talk to me in my head clear clear clear. She say, "Every Sunday I watch you sit down beside Miss Jonas with you face like when milk curdle. It no suit…" In case I wasn't sure is she, she say: "It no suit." Then I know. Sometime when she was alive and don't like something she say: "It DON'T suit" and emphasize the *Don't*. A frighten you see. The singing stop brap. She say, "People see you face set up so them will say Miss Jonas don't treat you good and you know that is not true. You must be all give the lady bad name already. You must pray about it. And I working on it for you. If you want good you nose haffi run. But nobody don't have to notice." She stop talking. And of course I didn't start back the singing. I feel me head spinning. I could hardly settle down. I find that I sweating although it not hot. When I catch myself I get up and pick a piece of broom weed, put it under mi tongue. They say that keep away spirit. Mind you I love my Granny, you know. But is the first time a spirit ever speak to me. That was the Thursday evening.

You want a tell you that same Thursday night Mrs. Johnson, Popsie Johnson mother, came over to the house. Me and Popsie was two of those that pass the Common Entrance for Knox College and we end up in the same form, so though we were not such good good friends in Grade six we sort of stick together in the new school. Well her mother come and ask Miss Jonas if she would let me go to Young People's night at their church. Is every Friday night but I could come that Friday and see if I like it. Miss Jonas say yes. I believe is Popsie tell her mother how I have to go with Miss Jonas to her church and how I sleep when I go.

That Friday I go to Young People's night. It don't mean that no big people not there, you know. Just that is a service with the young people in charge. Popsie church don't have any organ. It have piano and drum and tambourine. I started to wonder about myself if I am a cry cry person after all, because when I shake my body and jump to the tambourine I feel the tears coming to my eye.

Popsie and her mother take me back home safely. I sleep a little late the next morning but it was Saturday so no school. I tidy the house, wash my things, eat my lunch and settle down to home work. Miss Jonas ask what get into me, why I so sharp and chipsy. I tell her I don't know but I tell meself that maybe the sound of the tambourine still in me.

After that they come for me every Friday night. I say God is good.

I ask Miss Johnson if Popsie could come to church with me and Miss Jonas one Sunday. The truth is I want Popsie to see how the church really go because I wasn't sure she believe me. I ask Miss Jonas. She say, "Of course", so we drive pass Popsie house that Sunday morning on the way to church. Most of the time I find myself kicking her under the bench so she can notice some special parts like when the parson alone sing in that special way. When they pass around and say: "Peace be with You", Popsie laugh because I did warn her about it. I turn and laugh with her. Same time the fast woman come and put her hands out for peace with one big smile. I know she think I was smiling with her. I was laughing because Popsie could understand now what I was talking about.

Popsie want to know if I didn't want to come with her family on Sunday instead of putting up with that. We could ask Miss Jonas. I said "No", for I know how Miss Jonas pride herself on her church and she tell me from the first day I come to live with her that I have to go to church with her. And of course I remember Granny.

From that day things change. I find that every Sunday I can pretend that Popsie beside me and I kicking her foot under the bench. And I smile to myself. The fast woman I tell you about, now when she give me the peace, don't say "Smile", she just say "God loves you."

And now the priest want me to test out for choir. I don't know who tell him I can sing.

BIT

They called her "Bit" because when my father saw her he is supposed to have said, "What a little bit a pickni!" at which her mother perked up and said, "You want ar, Maas John?"

"Yes man, give ar to me noh."

"Mi serious you know sar."

"Why you want to give ar way?"

"A seven a dem mi have down a yaad you know sar an no faada."

My father says he hesitated briefly (no comment about the "no faada" business) and said, "Well I would have to ask Miss Margaret you know…"

I was already in boarding school then, getting ready to take my first really big examination so the news of a new arrival came to me by letter. My sister wrote:

> You will be surprised to hear that there is a baby in the house. A little half-Indian baby girl from Spring River. You know Papa was doing some work down there and a woman offered him this one. She has seven others and of course Mr. Kindhearted decided to add one to our two. And Mama said OK because she still has some of my baby clothes here (as if that is a good enough reason).

I got the impression that my sister, who was quite precocious for her eight years, was not too pleased. Nobody wants to give up the position of "baby" in a family especially without notice. If this had been Mama's child there would have been nine months at least, five from the time it started to show. Not so this time.

I didn't have to deal with it at all till Easter holidays.

Enid, who had been my sister's nanny, was mercifully unemployed and was glad to be rehired to care for this child. So there was really no extra pressure except on Mamma and Papa at night and I heard Mama tell her friends, "She is a good baby. Sleep through the night from I get her."

The holidays came and I was completely seduced by the tiny baby with the big eyes that took up half her face. I would take her for a walk in the mornings carefully wrapped up in a small blanket and would hear the stage whisper by passing adults: "A mirasmy baby you know". I had no idea what "mirasmy" was. I only knew from their behaviour that it was a disease people talked about in hushed tones. So I decided against asking my parents anything. Much much later I was to find a word in a psychology book: "Marasmus" and it said it meant lacking care and affection. The nutrition book said protein-energy malnutrition and sounded so confident I began to feel that the psychology meaning was a metaphorical take on it. I suppose the word in the vernacular applies irrespective of whether it is food or love you lack – or both.

Every morning Mr. Niggle's yardman delivered a pint of goat's milk to our house to be used in cornmeal porridge which Bit had at least twice per day. And to this day I vouch for cornmeal porridge. It can make children grow. It can make them healthy.

I fully expected the gossipers to say she was my child, that I had her in town and Miss Margaret decide to take it, and say is adoption. They did. Peunce found time to tell me she couldn't bear the suspense any more and I must tell her the truth. I said, "Yes, you know, Joshua is the father." Joshua is her brother who was also away at High School. There were no further questions, at least not any addressed directly to me.

She was christened Elizabeth Faith after church one "Parson Sunday", that is the fourth Sunday in each month when the Anglican priest came by car for the Office of Holy Communion and for christenings etc.. The other Sundays lay preachers took the service.

Eventually the distinction between "Bit" and "Beth" became blurred.

So people who knew her in High School called her Beth, but district people and those who had been in Elementary School called her Bit. Some district people still call her Miss Bit when she comes home.

You had to love this sweet-natured little baby puffing up your ego with her need for you. And we loved her. Even Yvonne, my sister, who had been resentful at first, quickly gave it up and joined in the adoration. By the time Bit started basic school Yvonne was competing with Enid to take her up the road to the clubhouse before school every morning. She didn't want anybody to help her carry the child. You could spot them a mile away, one head above the other, two well-shod feet hitting Yvonne's chest where breasts would soon be. A year later, Yvonne joined me at High School in town and Enid had Bit to herself, except for the wonderful holidays when we all were equals playing with her and jostling each other over star-apples at Easter and mangoes in the Summer.

Bit must have been ten or eleven, certainly not gone to high school yet, waiting in fact for the results of Common Entrance when the destabilizing thing happened. Apparently a group of boys who used to hang out on a culvert in a lonely part of the road home used to taunt her shouting, "Coolie Gal, a who a yu faada?" I forgot to mention that Bit had telltale long heavy curly hair, a challenge to comb in the mornings and quite different from mine or Yvonne's. We don't know how long it had been happening before my parents got wind of it. In fact it was when teary-eyed one afternoon she sat in her usual place at the foot of my father's rocking chair and asked, "Daddy, you are my father?" that it came out. Of course the question caught him unawares but he responded quickly: "Of course, why you ask?"

He wished the matter had come up another way. But it had to be dealt with. He picked her up from the foot of the rocking chair and put her on his lap.

"You are my daughter. You are our daughter. We chose you. It is true that you did not grow in Mama's belly, that I didn't put you there, but you are our child."

145

Tears were streaming down her face as she held on to him and hugged him tightly.

Papa told us that at the time she seemed less bothered about who her biological parents were than by the fact that she might not belong in the place where she had thought she belonged. He must have alerted Mama as soon as she came home because when Bit accosted her that night with, "So you are not even my mother, eh Mama!" she was ready.

"You are MY daughter though," she told her.

"I still want to know her."

"Who?"

"My real mother."

"I promise you that I will try my best to find her."

The road Papa had been building at Spring River had been finished by the time the formal adoption was done and he had never gone back there. I am not sure what went on in the weeks that followed. I know it involved Papa's going to Spring River and following a few leads as to where the lady with all those children had moved to. Having succeeded in getting the information he must have gone alone to the woman's house in Kingston at least once before the important journey after church one Sunday.

The woman lived on Slipe Pen Road near enough to Calvary cemetery. She occupied two rooms in a yard of eight rooms. Four of the children still lived with her.

Three boys and a girl. There was no man in sight. If there was one he might have been in the category "visitor" not "resident". One boy of about twelve must have had the same father as Bit because he looked so much like her. The others were all different from her and from each other. She said the two older children had left home. She did not elaborate.

Bit had wanted us all to be there for the meeting.

"Everybody coming in, don't it?" she had asked and we has answered in chorus, as if prearranged: "Of course."

It was a Sunday before a public holiday; I can't remember which one. That's how I came to be there.

Papa introduced her as Elizabeth and introduced the others of us.

The lady stepped forward to face Bit and said, "I am yu birt modda." She smiled. Bit held her head down first then looked up at her. I thought she was going to hug her but she just moved to the lady's side and squeezed her hand.

"I am glad to meet you," she said.

The other children had not been prepared for the encounter because they looked quite shocked when the woman said, "A yu sista, yu know."

I remember the whole episode as being very strange. At the end of it Papa said, "Now I know where you are we will keep in touch."

We went to an open-air restaurant on the way out of Kingston and had a nice lunch with cow-foot and beans and chicken and mackerel rundown. Everything. It was a buffet and we sat at a table under a nice shady tree. Everyone was strangely quiet. You could hear the gentle rush of water in the stream that ran below the rising where the tables were. If you looked down you could see the star-shaped tops of the river plants I call bulrushes, bending slightly at the touch of the water.

The normally talkative Bit wasn't saying a word.

Eventually she murmured almost under her breath:

"I don't remember any of them at all."

"How could you, my love?" Mama said. "You were three months old."

It wasn't long after that that Bit left for High School in Kingston. I went to London to do postgraduate studies and Yvonne lived in Mary Seacole Hall at the University at Mona. The headmaster at the elementary school had said she would go far. We didn't need him to tell us that. She read everything in sight and was extraordinarily inquisitive. It was clear that she would do something to do with writing. She got straight As in English from the first to the last report.

Excelsior had been a good choice for her. She was into every possible extracurricular activity. One school fair she was part of a fashion parade and caught the eye of a scout for models. By the time she was in third form she was earning money modelling on the weekend. She lived with Mrs. Grant, one of

Mama's friends, in Eden Gardens just behind the school and Mrs. Grant was modern, if vigilant.

I came back from London and settled into the long days and nights as a resident at the hospital. We seemed to be going our separate ways too quickly. My parents in desperation, instituted a fourth Sunday dinner at home so they could enjoy the company of their girls, they said. Fourth Sunday was Parson Sunday too so we could be expected to go to church and not complain about sermons by lay preachers.

Papa used to say that having children could not save you from loneliness because whether you had three or thirteen at some point they all go. He and Mama didn't look very lonely to me though. So many of those Sundays I had to beg a friend to work for me and give back the time another day. But I blessed that fourth Sunday meeting. There is no roast beef quite like the one that my mother puts on the table on Sunday. And the rice and peas, cooked in coconut milk, a thing unheard of in Kingston! And truly I enjoyed our being all together.

Bit got a scholarship to study journalism at Columbia University then went off to Brazil for a spell. She brought her brand new Brazilian husband back. He came to a research job in the Faculty of Social Sciences and she came to edit the journal the Faculty was responsible for, and to teach Portuguese 100. We had a big family party to welcome them and to sort of make up for the wedding reception we didn't get a chance to have.

Before they had settled down properly in the cottage on West Road there was a three month old baby girl with them. They called her Bita (remembering Claude McKay, Bit said). Before I could ask any questions she told me Bita was the child of one of the sisters from her birth family. There were already five of them. No father in sight so she took that one. I didn't say anything. I didn't think it was a good way to start a marriage but it wasn't my business. In any case, why wasn't I thinking of the child who was being given a chance? And how could Bit refuse? I wondered how they had managed to locate her so soon after their return, but then she had maintained contact all through her High School days. I used to suspect that all the money she got

148

from modelling went to her birth-mother. Of course I never asked.

The Brazilian husband seemed quite at ease with the arrangement. He told me about all the abandoned children in the favelas in Brazil, as if I had asked a question.

I thought of the sea turtles who lay their eggs on the shore and go back to sea cherishing the hope that even one will survive and make it to the deep. I imagined this mother saying later: "She is the one that get out. She grow with her aunt at the university."

"How many others did you say she has?" That was me to Bit.

"Five."

"And how old is she?"

"Twenty-five."

My silence was eloquent.

"Bit, it isn't my business, but go and talk to that woman about birth control and start talking to her daughters from now. This cycle have to break."

"Yes. I told her that if she has another one I am giving her back this one. And I am talking to her daughters. They young but is never too early and I am trying to make them stay in school.

I knew that that meant books and lunch money. But I could see two or three other turtles making it out to sea. I felt humbled and happy.

DEAD AND WAKE

A taxicab driving slowly from the entrance to the hospital was coming towards me. I hugged my side of the road. His entrance was my exit. I was going to the market.

"Where the dead-house?" the taximan shouted as I moved with caution over the sleeping policeman. "Over there," I said pointing to an area near the Pathology building. Then I could not close my mouth. It stayed open in shock as the taxi passed me. I was looking at a coffin strapped to the top of his cab. It was the most beautiful coffin I had ever seen. It wasn't a large one; surely for somebody less than five feet tall. It was painted a startling blue with dots of pink and orange. Eventually I stopped staring and drove on. But very slowly.

A student nurse was emerging from the hostel gate. "Young lady," I said, "please tell me where the morgue is." She pointed in the same direction I had indicated to the taximan. I felt comforted. I hadn't misdirected him. I wondered whether the young woman and I would both lose our fingers for pointing in the direction of the coffin. I wasn't sure whether the rule applied to empty coffins or only to occupied ones. To be on the safe side I bit my thumb. I was old enough to know that that would prevent it from rotting. I asked the young woman if she had ever heard about that practice. She laughed and, predictably, said no.

I had never before seen or even imagined a coffin strapped to the roof of a car. I kept marvelling at the phenomenon as I went on my way. I kept seeing not so much the taximan's face as that of the woman who had been staring at me through the passenger window. Her face was shine and round with bright determined eyes. I am not sure why I decided she was the godmother of the deceased and was going to identify the body, a task too painful for the biological mother or father. I kept thinking how much heavier the taxi would be when the coffin did contain the corpse. Dead people, even dead children, are supposed to be so heavy. Dead animals, too, of course. That is the significance of dead as opposed to live weight in discussions about the cost of chicken, for example. So much for all of that. I was on my way to buy my week's supply of fruit and vegetables.

I try never to return by the same route I have come, if I can help it. I am not sure why. Something positive about going in circles perhaps. So on my way from the market I took Old Hope Road instead of passing through the hospital. I was cruising down there only to notice, just as I was about to turn at the traffic light to enter Mona Heights, a crowd and a police car parked nearby. This was very unusual for a Saturday morning. I did a left turn, then a little right, so as not to incur the wrath of any of the law men, and I parked.

I climbed up the bank so I could look over and saw, in the street, a girl of about nine, in a pink nightgown lying in a foetal position. I recognized the "godmother" lady from the taxi. She was fanning the young girl. There were splinters of wood scattered about, blue with pink and orange dots, obviously broken from the coffin. The taxi driver was shouting angrily at a man who seemed to be the driver of a small truck that was parked a little way off the road. The empty, topless coffin was lying on its side. The two policemen on the scene had no difficulty containing the crowd. They were all too frightened to carry on at the decibel level at which Jamaican crowds usually perform.

The girl's toes were moving and people in the crowd were pointing at them. The godmother alternately fanned the face and pressed a handkerchief on the brow of the young girl. It was clear what had happened. The impact of truck on taxi had hurled the coffin from its position. Whether the strapping had not been tight enough and which driver was wrong were, by then, mere academic questions interesting only to the taxi driver, the truck man and perhaps the police.

The young girl had been thrown awake from the coffin. Someone in the crowd whispered "Dead an wake." I stared shamelessly at the girl.

I remembered how Miss Becka, years before, had been brought home to our village from Port Maria hospital amid great singing and wailing and how when the makeshift coffin was taken from the truck at the foot of her hill, she had groaned "Mmm" and lived to see many other people's coffins. I had not seen Miss Becka then. I had only heard the shocking report. I was certainly too young to have been out there with the adults in the night. But that morning I saw Dead and Wake. They would take her back to the hospital. I had a feeling she would live to be a very old woman.

Dead and Wake wouldn't leave me. Maybe I just wanted to be in on whatever would become of her because I was sure she had been spared for some special reason. Monday afternoon I went to Ward 16 where older children stay. I glanced through the back window and spotted her immediately. I went to the front desk and asked the nurse in charge if I could visit the girl in bed 8. "Of course," she said. They weren't half as strict there as in the rest of the hospital. She was alone. I gave her the third degree. Not for any sinister reason. I wanted to get books to read to her, so I needed to find out a few things. Her name was Natasha Lindo, lived with her grandparents Jim and Elizabeth Lindo. Went to Dunrobin Primary. Grade five getting ready to go to grade six with Common Entrance hanging over her life. Liked to play with her friends and read (Bible) stories.

I returned in the evening with *The Sun's Eye*. It was a good choice. The stories are short. I figured she might be able to read some of them herself when she was strong enough to sit up for long periods. I started with a poem "Jamaica Market". She was smiling and following me in whispers.

"You know this one then," I said.

"Yes. When I was in grade four, a lady came to my class to teach us for a few weeks and that is one of the poems we had to learn."

"You want to hear something else?"

"Yes, Mam."

I chose "Linda's Bedtime" by Andrew Salkey. It would soon be her bedtime. I had barely finished the first paragraph when an older woman came towards the bed.

"That is my grandmother."

I rose and introduced myself, lying that I belonged to a group that read to sick children.

She thanked me and took out a thermos-flask with chicken soup. I recognized the face. It was the same round face with the determined eyes I had seen in the taxi.

I went outside and sat on the edge of the concrete wall that surrounded the little garden in front of the ward. The lie stuck in my throat. I NEVER read stories for sick children. That was the first time. Suddenly it seemed like the most natural thing to do. I decided that I would continue to do it and that I would try to form a group, to live up to my lie, sort of. Perhaps I could check students who lived on the university campus near the hospital. They could take turns, making sure somebody came every evening. It came back to me that when I was a young woman a group of us from the campus used to go to the Polio Centre on a Friday to sing, read, play games and generally interact with the disabled children.

There was a lot of coming and going to observe while I waited on Grandma to feed Natasha. A woman sat across from me, on the other side of the concrete edge.

She smiled at me. I smiled back. She obviously wanted to talk. I had taken it for granted that she was supervising children while their mothers went into the ward to visit a sick brother or sister. There were four children at her side and a lame one on her shoulder. She wanted to talk. I had to listen. She had brought her brood to the hospital she said, so she could expose them to what suffering was. I asked her about the risk to them of catching some disease. I thought that children who were well were not allowed in hospitals. She said she didn't take them in the ward. She didn't go further than the verandah. While I was pondering this strange behaviour she moved herself and the children to a long table a few feet away, to the place she called the verandah. The penny dropped when I saw food being brought to the verandah and all the ambulatory children rushing out to take their places at the table. The visiting children moved up to the table and the woman moved closer, still holding the lame child. Everybody ate. It seems that the

153

nurse or nurse's aide, or whoever organized the feeding, understood and allowed it. I was in a state of shock. Clearly this woman had come to a feeding tree and had simply given me that story to hold. Serve me right. Who could believe such a thing?

After dinner she didn't go away. She sent the two older children into the ward to join the sick children in front of the TV. Grandma waved to me. She was leaving. I went back to finish my story and stayed until the nurse came to give Natasha her night medication.

Back home I was confused. I was upset. I telephoned my friends: church, laity, social workers – anybody who should be touched. The woman with the batch of children coming for food and entertainment at the hospital was a prototype signifying something I had never faced before. Would some church agree to set up a homework centre in Kingvalley, the area the woman said she came from? Would the Lions or some other service club furnish the building if the church found one?

After dinner my head was clear. Putting a homework centre in Kingvalley would help the woman I saw that day near the ward. What about other children not from there? When I had talked with the nurse about my horror and concern, she only made it worse by telling me they had to keep a close watch on non-ambulatory children who did not want to eat or ate too slowly. Visiting children invariably stole their food. So Kingvalley couldn't be the answer. Not all the visiting children came from there. Some genuinely came to visit brothers and sisters. What they had in common was that they were hungry. They could do with a place where they could get something to eat, legitimately, and perhaps do some homework, if they went to school, and yes, watch TV. So a recreation/homework centre that served a snack was what they needed.

I never discovered what had caused Natasha to pass for dead. I will never know whether she would have awakened had she not fallen from the coffin. I only know that I made sure that every evening of the three months she stayed in the ward, somebody came to read to her and talk to her. After the second week she was able to do some exercises from the verbal reasoning and English books her grandmother brought. Some Sundays children from her class came by with their parents. Her teacher came a few times when I was there and we talked. She was a bright little girl and would surely pass the Common Entrance. She wanted to go to Queens or St. Hughs. When she was able she started going around the ward visiting other children. The nurses said she was their little helper.

Today, when I enter Ward Sixteen from the verandah I see the brightly painted container converted to the Natasha Lindo Centre. I know that children are sitting in there looking at TV. They will have finished their homework or listened to a story read by a young volunteer. They will have had a snack of some sort: a sandwich and a drink perhaps. Or a hot dog, a piece of chicken and a roll or a patty – depending on whether Burger King or Mothers or Kentucky Fried was the sponsor of the evening.

The women who brought them are sitting on the edge of the same concrete circle I sat on that first evening. Each of them is doing something: repairing a hem, making hand-stitched pot-holders or other small craft items. Some evenings profession-als, who were willing to give time, talk to them about various aspects of child-care. You would be surprised to know the simple, helpful hints they had never heard – like how to prevent your child from getting dehydrated before you reach a doctor if you suspect gastro.

I didn't do it all myself. All I had was the idea. When I started to ask for help I got it immediately and in abundance, as if people were simply waiting to be asked to do something. I keep in touch with Natasha. She is at University now, on a scholarship. She is one of the students going over to read for sick children. All the nurses she knew have moved on. One of the doctors is still there and gives her a big smile whenever they meet. Her colleagues don't know about her relationship to the centre. They know her as Genevieve Lindo. Natasha is her middle name and the one they use at home.

And to think it all started when a coffin fell off the top of a taxi one Saturday morning on Hope Road.

JACKET

It was still dark when *The Conquistador* dropped anchor at the wharf on Isabel. Just five o'clock and the few stars ridiculously clear. Straight ahead was the sign we had been told to look for – "Panaderia de Ana" – and old men were already milling about waiting. And there was that aroma… the unmistakeable smell of bread in the oven baking…

The door opened and the baker man spat out "Pan solo", through a crack. Those who wanted only bread edged closer to receive their half-pound or one-pound warm paperbag of *sobao*, the bread made with lard (as opposed to *agua* without it). Those of us who wanted the piping hot coffee with our warm bread stood back.

Nothing smells quite like hot bread newly baked. The smell covered the air past us all the way back to the wharf. Soon we received our bread and coffee, though with no hint of a smile or the accustomed "*buen provecho*" from this bakerman. We started walking up the road, tearing the bread between sips of coffee as we walked past shutters still tight, protecting eyes that need not wake too soon. No work to go to in a place where the government owns two thirds of the island, the sugar factories gone and no industry to replace it.

Old men would still be sitting at the same tables much much later when we passed again for coffee. Solo.

I had no idea what to expect from this island but after we had walked through the main streets of the town I knew what I didn't expect. I didn't expect a place that showed so little sign of having been owned by Spain. A plaza yes, but no houses with little balconies no cobble-stoned streets. Isabel looked like a George had settled it. America wouldn't have used Havana nor

San Juan for whatever dangerous manoeuvre the citizens had recently been protesting. Those places had been made pretty by Spain and had been kept pretty by the US. Not even God loves ugly. Maybe Isabel wasn't born ugly, but it had been made so by a series of historical circumstances. Then the same people who made it ugly started treating it like Cinderella (before the Prince). Isn't that always the story?

It was beginning to lighten when we reached the gate. The descriptions had been precise. We walked up a steep street, took a right turn and came to a plateau facing two extravagantly large houses which I thought might be drug lords' houses. The newspapers the day before had reported something about a drug bust and the police.

The little house, painted a discreet beige, sat on the plateau overlooking the sea. On the gatepost hung a miniature vintage black Ford above a sign which read "In the beginning…" A tiny dark green verandah went all the way round and two hammocks were slung, one at each end of the part that faced the sea. The gate was open. We walked straight through the yard without calling out and were gazing in wonder at the sea spread out in an unruffled blue in the still cool morning.

"Hi there!"

That was Jim taking his head briefly from the frying pan and the stove to greet us. The smell of great coffee brewing was in the air and certainly my stomach started contracting in expectation, in spite of the so recent cup.

I threw my bag to the ground and sat on a chair in the shade of the largest tree in the yard. There is this about holidays that there is never any hurry about anything. I noted that the tree was a guinep (chennet) tree and started thinking about the hordes of school children who would jump the fence to invade when the school, in construction across the way, opened. There was a big sign announcing it. I tried to rock back on the chair and found that it was firmly tied to the tree.

"Dona Celia," I shouted, "Good Morning. Come tell me why the chair is tied."

"Because of the wind," she replied. I tried to imagine wind that could move a chair but didn't wish to continue the

157

conversation at that distance. In any case I could hear a calypsonian (was it Kitchener? Didn't sound like him. Definitely not Sparrow) singing in my early sixties' head:

Good morning, Miss Santa living here?
Yes yes is she
Now a lady bring a report to me
that you tiif she man from shi
an as a poliis is mi bounden duty
to sue you for larceny
You see, Santa tiif a big man from St. James
and tie him like a cow out in Morvant

Sun and rain wetin di man
an he can't get away poor fella

I started singing along with the calypsonian. "What's that?" Celia called out. "A calypso" I replied, thinking that obviously the difference between my speech and my singing was not as clear as I thought it was.

Breakfast was announced. Coffee and hot rolls and of course fruit. Now I asked for a further explanation about the tied-up chair and rendered "Miss Santa" for them. The conversation moved to the humour in calypso and eventually to a lecture by me on the pun in the verb "tie" and the notion of a woman tieing a man by various means, sometimes with the help of an obeah man.

The fickle Caribbean man came up for scrutiny. The conclusion was that one only goes to such lengths when the men find commitment difficult. Was it any wonder, though, when the same verb for commitment describes the act of sentencing by the judge... "I commit you to ten years hard labour" or something like that. OK blame the language again then blame colonialism, then slavery...

"You will soon experience the wind," Celia said, "then you won't laugh."

"Well, why not simply take the chair inside when it is not in use?"

158

She gave me a long story. She had this old man friend (over ninety) who liked to visit her. She wanted him to feel welcome even in her absence. In my mind I saw a decrepit old man, stooped, slowly making his way to the plateau and slumping down into the chair.

We had barely finished breakfast when they all opted to go to the sea. All but me, not only because I had been taught that the sea immediately after a meal was unhealthy but because I felt tired and I could do with the peace and aloneness. I would have a chance to enjoy, perhaps to finish, the fat book I was reading.

An hour or so later I heard the measured kung kung of a cane and looked out. A tall, elegant, well-built and well-dressed older man was approaching. He could be seventy I thought. But he went to sit in the leashed chair and I realized that this was the ninety-year-old friend. No stoop. No wrinkles. I didn't want him to know that anyone was at home. I continued my reading but soon felt my eyes closing down. I was fighting sleep.

I woke up with a start and saw my book on the rug at the bedside. I was frightened. An old woman had dreamed me. Had elected to come to me while I slept. I didn't know her. She had put her fingers on her lips to silence me and had begun her tale:

"Is her father you know. But she don't know and him don't know. Me name Susan. Them used to call me Ma Sue. Him an me was play mate. If me was alive me would be ninety-one. Me and him go to school in Tortola. That is where I come from. His father was a doctor over there. All these islands mix up. A lot of travelling from one to the other used to go on. I married and come to live over here. My husband was a sugar boiler. Those was estate days. Dead some ten years before me. This one here was a teacher working in St. Croix. Married a Crucian woman. But I did always have a soft spot for him. Him like this island. Now Celia, her parents live in St. Thomas, but they used to come over here to spend time with family every holiday. For years they didn't have any children. He, the man, used to teach school over here every year in the Summer. The Catholic church used to run the programme for poor children who weren't doing so well in school.

Seem like the man didn't like the water. Was a very light skin man so maybe the sun used to bother him. The mother was a richer colour and she love the water. This man here… Tell you the truth, I used to watch him because although both of us married, my feelings never change. Always have a soft spot for him. From the Tortola days. Of course, with what colour is in these islands I know I didn't have a chance. But you know woman like to punish themself. Anyway this day I happen to be in a little place across the bay. You can see the cove from there. This afternoon him must be finish teach and decide to go enjoy the water and for some reason she was there. I can't tell you all that take place. She was a very pretty woman, you know. Firm body. And he was very handsome. You can still see that now. There is something they call electric attraction. Well, that catch them. They sit down in the cove talking. I don't know what they was talking about or how it happen, I only know I see him start kiss her. Next thing him was taking the bathing suit off her shoulders and kissing her breast. Well from one thing to the other… Then I couldn't look any more. My two knee was shaking too hard. Jealous and everything. And a find myself worrying, suppose she get pregnant…

Well anyway, when she and the husband come back the next August she have this little girl. Dead stamp of the mother. The husband proud him proud him proud so till. Him stop stick up in the house and walking all over the place with this little girl. Of course, they continue the annual summer visits. This break her duck, and she had two more children, two boys. But this little girl she love this place everlasting. Every chance she get she come over here. And now with the husband. Build up this little house. They not too long married. See them call the house the beginning. Mean them just starting real life…

Years ago she meet up this old man, for him retire over here. Since the wife die, him didn't have to stay in St. Croix. And is so she love him, so him love her. But none of them don't suspect a thing. I go to my grave with the secret but as a hear you asking about the chair I decide is you I should tell."

The regular kung kung of the stick indicated that the old man

160

was leaving. I peeped at him through the window. I had never had a vision before. I hoped I would never have another one. Eventually the crowd returned. Hungry. Again. The sea does that. There was ready made pasta in the fridge. I got up and washed my face.

"Your old man friend was here," I said.

"I'm so sorry I missed him. He was interesting eh! Did he tell you any stories?"

"I didn't talk to him, you know. Didn't want to disturb him. Just peeped at him and wondered how many ninety-year-olds look like that."

"You should see him dance meringue and bolero!"

I was laughing like everybody else, but I was scrutinizing Celia's face and her figure for something of the old man. There was nothing. Her heavy black hair sat on her shoulders as if a crane would have to lift it. His grey hair had been blowing as he went down the hill exposing the few light-brown strands that were left.

"Dead stamp of her mother," I heard Ma Sue say in my head.

In a sudden flash I realized where I had seen Ma Sue before. It was the face in a portrait in the brochure from the ticket office for the ferry to come over. Portrait of a freed woman in late slavery years, copy of the original in the local Museum-cum-Art Gallery.

I remembered that when I asked, they had told me there was no word in their language for what in my Creole we call "Jacket", in another, "Ready-made shirt". The community does not recognize, so the language does not need to have a word for the concept of a child born to a woman not from the seed of her husband.

ABOUT THE AUTHOR

Velma Pollard was born in Jamaica in 1937, educated at Excelsior High School in Kingston and at the University College of the West Indies. She received an MA in Education from McGill University and an MA in the teaching of English from Columbia University. She taught in high schools and universities in Jamaica, Trinidad, Guyana and the USA. Since 1975 she taught at the University of the West Indies, Mona. She retired as Senior Lecturer in Language Education and Dean of the Faculty of Education of the University of the West Indies.

She has always written. She won her first prize for a poem at the age of seven, but none of her work went beyond her desk until 1975 when encouraged by her sister Erna Brodber and others, notably Jean D'Costa who sent one of her stories to *Jamaica Journal*, she started sending pieces to journals in the region. She published *Crown Point and Other Poems*, *Shame Trees Don't Grow Here* and *Leaving Traces* with Peepal Tree in 1988, 1992 and 2008 respectively. *Considering Woman*, a collection of prose pieces was published by The Women's Press in 1989. Her novella *Karl* won the Casa de las Americas in 1992. Her monograph, *Dread Talk - the Language of the Rastafari* was published in 1994 by Canoe Press. She has also edited several anthologies of writing for schools.

She is the mother of three children.

Crown Point
ISBN: 9780948833243; pp. 84; £7.99

Crown Point is the first and long overdue collection of poems
by one of the Caribbean's foremost woman poets. Velma
Pollard's poems range from affectionate and observant family
portraits to the righteous anger of an Afro-Caribbean woman's
truth telling. *Crown Point* closes with a moving series of poems
that meditate on death, mourning and their meaning for the
living. They speak both of the deaths of parents and grandparents and of 'deaths falling early' and hear always Anancy's susu
susu whispering words, 'tiday fi mi/ tumaro fi yu'. These are
poems which have a quiet, consoling truthfulness, no answers,
just the unvarnished reminder that this is the way of life and
that the dead remain with us: 'No one philosophy can answer
all/ each man is an island/ each mind is a muffin tin/ and so we
sit with our invisible pencils/ working out strategies to cope
with brevity/ to cope with our adieux/ to love - too sweet to
forget/ to life - too intense to leave...' These tender elegiac
poems of loss and remembrance have an eloquent stillness at
their heart. All share a common depth of reflection and
concern with poetic craft.

'Reading... Velma Pollard is to encounter an acutely sensitive
consciousness grappling, even in apparently lighter moments,
with the complexity of experience.' - Evelyn O'Callaghan,
Jamaica Journal

Shame Trees Don't Grow Here, but Poincianas Bloom
ISBN: 9780948833489; pp. 72; £7.99

A shame tree is a Jamaican symbol for the development of
moral consciousness, and the poems in this collection explore
the points at which moral values emerge - and the conse-
quences of their absence. The poems suggest toughly that such
consciousness does not grow without unremitting effort and

scrupulous sensitivity to feeling, but there is nothing didactic or moralistic about them. They are imaginative recreations of the dramas of coming to consciousness and the inevitable ambiguities of truth. As in all Velma Pollard's work, there is a deeply imbued sense of Caribbean history.

Marvin Williams writes in *The Caribbean Writer*: 'Tone and emotion range wider in Velma Pollard's *Shame Trees Don't Grow Here... but poincianas bloom* - from disgust, anger, and outrage to celebration, awe, and praise; from questioning and condemnation to understanding and reconciliation. The major thrust of the poet's fire comes in the first part of the book where those who lacked or are lacking conscience and moral boundaries are drawn into Pollard's unflinching scrutiny. Wildfire becomes hearth in part two where the beauty and life-enhancing qualities of land, sea, and people are celebrated. Throughout, the poet's skillful use of language remains evident in, for example, her subtle, unobtrusive rhymes that lend musicality to her verse; her puns; double entendres; and other word play.'

Leaving Traces
ISBN: 9781845230210; pp. 88; £8.99

Velma Pollard has developed a significant following among her fellow Jamaicans and in the wider Caribbean world. In this collection she will delight these — and new readers — with her capacity to unite the personal and the political in a seamless whole. Organized into three sections, the collection explores underlying political concerns, such as the impact of global culture, the dangers of unobstructed American power, and the threat of Islamist opposition. The poems move beyond these problems, however, ultimately seeking resolution through understanding the flow of nature and urging a celebration of life.

All Peepal Tree titles are available from the website:
www.peepaltreepress.com